MYTHIC

Also by Mike Allen

DEFACING THE MOON
PETTING THE TIME SHARK
DISTURBING MUSES
STRANGE WISDOMS OF THE DEAD

As editor:

NEW DOMINIONS:
FANTASY STORIES BY VIRGINIA WRITERS

THE ALCHEMY OF STARS:
RHYSLING AWARD WINNERS SHOWCASE
(with Roger Dutcher)

MYTHIC

edited by
Mike Allen

Mythic
Delirium
Books

MYTHIC 2

Published by Mythic Delirium Books
http://www.mythicdelirium.com
in cooperation with Prime Books
http://www.prime-books.com

Contents

*Old myths, old gods, old heroes have never died.
They are only sleeping at the bottom of our mind,
waiting for our call. We have need for them.
They represent the wisdom of our race.*

— Stanley Kunitz

Sonya Taaffe
Homecoming

Hold me down: deeper, till I forget
there is air that your mouth does not filter
to mine, red-gilled, in drowning salt,
bitterness seeping between our lips
like the tears I will never see you cry.

There is no rapture of the deep. There is no siren's
sweet, sad promise, that the wind carries farther than the
sight of sun-leathered bones, no honey-lipped lure that has
set fast before the first downward tug reaches your heart.
I run the water cold into the tub, claw-footed, iron-bellied,
antique as the prints you have hung on the walls: green
depths, pale mermaid's flesh, endless hair that rays out
into a net where fisherman entangle themselves and
drown. I measure salt into my palm, handfuls for sea and
table, Kirke with her poisons that she poured into the
waves. There is only me, with hands too warm and mortal
for your tastes, too fragile and unclawed, unwebbed, to
finish your desires. There is only the sunlight, as I lean
over to turn off the tap, rippling beneath me on the water
like a lie.

Keep me under: longer, till I remember
the sting of your stickleback fingers,
anemone-nailed, your hair that slithered
like weed in the dimness, twining us
slickly fast: and not binding enough.

When you washed up on the shore, onto fractured mussel shells and tide-tangles of kelp, another discard from the sea's careless, bottomless hoard, I ran to the hospital in yesterday's jeans and barefoot, sure I would find a corpse — strangled so blue, thumbprinted like a suicide, scraped and torn as though shale and granite and scouring shingle had chewed on you and spat you back. Your eyes were blank as a sleepwalker's. There was dark sand under your tongue. Wrapped in blankets, you shivered like a feverish child, restless, unspeaking, and stared out the passenger's side window all the drive home. As we turned up the driveway, you twisted to follow the last glimpse of the night sea, the industrial lights floating on the harbor like foam. Did you hear me call your name? You were deafened not to the sirens, but to the world they had fled.

> Drown me in you: forever, till I am lost
> in your breasts as rough as barnacles,
> the taut and luminous fins that parted
> to let me enter, secret as pearl, what I
> abandoned for this harsh and miserly land.

You lie in the water like Ophelia's model, like Melusine drifted off and drowned some Saturday afternoon. Do you think I will not notice the scars, slit pink beneath the hinge of your jaw? Do you think I cannot see the bruises in the cradle of your throat? Marks that my hands did not leave, but I still make a fist of my fingers knotted in your wet hair, thumbnail turned edge-on into the starved curve of your hip, still the bitter water shocks my wrists. I cannot sing. The bathroom is bright with late morning, no abyss in white tile and bathmats and the chipped conch shell you placed on the windowsill like a sentinel. Faintly, through the resonances of tapwater and iron, I hear you humming.

8

Let me die in you, the true and final time:
let the barbs of your tongue and frigid teeth
devour me, let your self-lit darkness hide
me from the earth. Let your sea-cave hold
my homecoming. Let your song stop my ears.

Under my hands, under the cold and salted water that never came from the sea, you shudder and struggle against my no more than human strength and the air floods glassily from your nose and mouth. Did I wait for this, scan horizon and harbor like a sea-captain's widow, call police and paramedics and pray to gods I had never believed in before? Did I think you would come back unchanged? There is real salt in the tub now, tears, but you will never taste them. There are only a few seconds between little death and greater. There are so many different kinds of dark. Oh, my sea-scarred love. I will not let you drown.

Charles Saplak
Visanna

V ISANNA STOOD BEFORE THE MIRROR in her tower room, staring at the face which she wouldn't wear tomorrow. Occasionally she moved her head from side to side, catching glimpses of the twenty-six other faces which moved behind her like the time-lapse tail of a strange, slow comet.

Of course Visanna still would possess the face which she had now; she just wouldn't be wearing it. At midnight it would move back to take its place in front of the twenty-six others, and a new face would appear on the front of her head — herself as a twenty-eight year old.

In the light cast by the leviath oil lamps in their iron sconces she examined the face one last time, then adjusted the tight braids in her long blonde hair. She tugged gently at the lace sleeves of her gown, then practiced gesturing to make sure that the crocheted webs of black silk and golden thread which connected the gown's wrists to its sides would move naturally and not tangle.

As she gestured she whispered to the mirror.

"Simply marvelous, Duchess Harrian."

"What an interesting observation, General Cho."

"You flatter me, Lord and Lady . . . ?"

And with that, whether she had failed to think of a name or whether she had tired of the rehearsal, she dropped her arms and, frowning, continued to examine her dress. Everything was in order. The jewelry she wore was arranged exactly as prescribed: the ruby pin above the left breast signifying that she was a soldier's wife; a small amulet of lapis lazuli signifying that her father had been of the Technician Caste, the amulet suspended by a slender chain of white gold, signifying that she was married but childless.

All is as it should be, Visanna noted silently, turning away from the mirror. *Everything is in its place.*

Her private tower room was as in any traditional Kavonian castle. Built on a semicircular plan and separated by a straight wall from her husband's semicircular private room, it had three large windows, the glasses of which could be retracted by geared handles. Visanna crossed the room and sat on the ledge of the center window.

The sun was westering; it made the landscape as far as she could see crisp and long-shadowed. To the far west were the Meisterilein Mountains; next were the verdant hills of the Cobweb Forest; closer still were the cultivated lands around the border of the city; and then the slate-roofed cottages and shacks which jumbled together, sometimes coming right up to the walls of her husband's estate and castle.

In the courtyard below was a shallow pool. Visanna stared into the shimmering waters which reflected the orange and purple of the evening sky. She noticed something moving in the water, and for a moment imagined that it was one of the magical fish or frogs which appeared in fairy tales to offer gifts to princesses. Next she thought it was a pale bird walking on a ledge which protruded from the tower wall. Looking more intently, she realized that she was seeing her own reflection; her current face and the faces of her younger selves which trailed behind her like jealous ghosts looking over her shoulder.

It could have been them calling to her in a strange voice which seemed to simultaneously taunt and warn and plead, "Visanna, Visanna, Visanna, ..."

But in fact it was her husband in the circular marriage chamber below, calling to tell her it was time to leave for the party, his steady voice echoing and distorting as it touched the stone walls of the tower.

THE RIDE TO THE CASTELLATED HOME of Duchess Harrian was quiet, save for the metallic claws of the chimerasaur team and the carriage wheels on the cobblestones.

Artran, Visanna's husband, sat beside her, resplendent in his Lieutenant's dress uniform, his miniature medals (including the Disc of Valor awarded him during the Chaurenian War) adorning his left breast below the golden sword-and-stirrup device which marked him as a cavalry officer.

Visanna examined his faces. His head was slightly turned so he could look out the carriage window at the sights on the way. He regarded the beggars who sat against moss-encrusted walls like bony heaps; the merchants who held up hammered metal jewelry and bottled spices and intricately woven fabrics while they chanted prices at passersby; at the bored soldiers who wandered the streets in search of diversions.

Artran watched without expression. His face could have been chiseled from stone; every face behind him was a regular and balanced component of his life. He was a man of orderly progression.

Their marriage, of course, had been an arranged one.

"Visanna, you're staring at me," Artran said.

Her reverie broken, she blushed and stammered.

"I was curious, my Lord. I wondered what you found so fascinating in the streets of the city."

He smiled wryly. "Kavone at peace. The nation of Chauren has been deconstructed, its legislatures discredited and its armies routed. Who will profit from this latest war?"

His voice, like his faces, was emotionless.

Visanna held her silence.

Artran changed the subject. "Do be polite with the Duchess Harrian, my love."

Visanna scowled, and faces behind her showed the faintest traces of echoing expressions. "She makes me feel like a flower. She moves through her parties like some great, monstrous gardener among her tiny flowers. She dotes, but I fear that she might reach down with her fingernails and pinch off an ear, or my nose, or some fingers, as if pruning a plant. All for my own good, you understand."

"Tolerate her, Visanna," Artran said softly. "For some reason I can't fathom any more than you can, the Duke and Duchess are considered to be important."

"Is there any good reason for the party this evening?" Visanna asked.

Artran shrugged. "The Duchess promised fascinating things; strange and memorable sights."

THE HARRIAN FAMILY MANSION exhibited the same characteristics which Visanna most closely associated with the Duchess herself: in bulk and dimension it was large beyond reason, occupying a full city block. Like all of the structures which had survived from the days when battles were fought on Kavonian soil into the current historical period, it exhibited curious architectural holdovers. For example, the roof's edge was ringed with elaborate gargoyles whose mouths could serve as machicillations for pouring hot oil on seigers — but these days they were decorated with gay flags and fresh arrangements of country flowers. Likewise, certain corners of the mansion were supported by seventy-foot-tall caryatids, representations of Meisterileinien cave-dwelling monsters, the surfaces of which held iron spikes on which many a storm trooper had bled to death hundreds of years ago — but these days they were more likely to be covered not with rotting corpses but with ceremonial banners and jade-colored vines.

A groom, wearing an elaborate but threadbare ceremonial costume, took the lead chimerasaurs by their bridles and led them clattering away into the estate stables.

"Careful with those beasts, son," Artran called.

The youth nodded in reply. "They'll not fight, sir; they'll be well cared," the footman called back.

Artran took Visanna by the left arm. She felt slender and fragile in his large right hand.

"Good cheer, my flower," he whispered, eliciting a nervous smile. The sounds of music and laughter; the smells of incense and roasted meat; the gay light of lanterns set in mirrored webs; these things poured into the night.

Together they ascended the stairs to the mansion of Family Harrian.

DUCHESS HARRIAN GREETED THEM personally. Visanna cringed as the woman approached.

The banquet hall was immense, but the Duchess filled it. The mirrored lamps and roasting fires were blinding, but the Duchess outshone them. The resonance of the strings and reeds caressed into music by the savant musicians in their cages was throbbing, but the Duchess drowned it out.

"Oh, it is our Artran, our heroic Artran," the Duchess sang as she clasped Artran's right hand between her own huge, meaty hands.

"You honor us with your invitation, Duchess Harrian," Artran said, steadily and with minimal expression.

The Duchess tilted her head back and to one side so she could cry out, "The Chaurenian War was not over until you returned; and our party had not begun until you arrived."

Artran nodded politely, Visanna noticed, the faces of his former selves bobbing as if to echo the sentiment of their living replacement.

And then the Duchess turned to Visanna, who steeled herself in preparation. She caressed Visanna's cheeks and turned the smaller woman's head upward so she could look into her eyes. The Duchess's hands were heavily scented with something which reminded Visanna of the fragrance of moonsigh blossoms, and the palms were slick with perspiration.

"Our Visanna. Our sweet child. Artran's wonderful wife," the Duchess cooed. Her voice was musical, but her gaze pierced Visanna like grey steel needles.

"And you, our child," the Duchess continued. "Soon to be no longer a child. Soon to be no longer amazed by the world. You are lucky to be with us, Visanna, just as we are lucky to have you."

"We are honored, of course, Duchess Harrian," Visanna said, meekly. She felt as if the life force were flowing out of her into the larger woman's hands.

"There will be fascinations here tonight," the Duchess said, her eyes darting from Visanna's face to Artran's, then back again. "We will see marvelous things tonight, our children, I promise you that."

Visanna, when released by the Duchess, had to clutch at Artran's arm in order to not fall to the floor.

* * *

AS THE DUCHESS TURNED AWAY Visanna stared at the line
of faces — they numbered more than sixty — which trailed
behind the woman's head. Even in the days when the
Duchess's face had been unlined and youthful it still had a
hungry, forceful, but slightly befuddled look.

Visanna looked at the expressions in the eyes of the
past faces, and realized that, like the Duchess's long line of
faces, which bobbled along behind her with dim echoes of
her expressions fleeting across their aspect, the Duchess
herself was not entirely engaged with the people around
her. She moved among her guests — now greeting a couple,
now touching the arm of a man and tugging him toward a
woman, now making a great show of laughing at some joke
— but she was removed from the reality of the world
around her.

We are all scenery to her, Visanna thought.

AT ONE POINT EARLY IN THE PARTY, a parade of attendants
entered with strange birds in iron cages. The jewel-plumed
birds had been captured at great risk from their nests high
in the sheer cliffs of the Meisterilein Mountains.

The crowd fell quiet as the cages were hung from hooks
on tall metal poles; the savant musicians all set down their
instruments.

The birds, one by one, began to sing; their songs
banished the silence.

The people in the crowd stole glances at one another,
and gradually began breathing in time to the song the birds
were weaving. (Visanna felt as if she were the tiniest,
simplest thread in a great tapestry which was draped over
the throne of an unimaginable and dreadfully uncaring
titan.)

The savant musicians, themselves in cages, leaned

16

forward and tilted their heads from side to side, in order to listen more analytically to the birdsong.

And the song was woven tighter and tighter around the throng of revelers, who stood swaying and rocking to the rhythms. Attendants took the cages from their hooks and carried them toward the braziers.

LATER, VISANNA'S ATTENTION was drawn to one particular woman who picked delicately at the flesh of roasted bird. She was stunningly beautiful, with slick black hair woven into a complex braid; with light blue eyes, pale skin, and translucent teeth.

But Visanna looked behind the woman and saw the faces of her past selves. Yes, going back only a few years one saw the same exquisitely sculpted features and mysterious, calm expressions, but if one looked far enough back one could see the earliest faces. No, this woman had not always been beautiful! Far back in her past her faces were sallow and thin, her eyes ringed round with the crimson of pain and the gray of fatigue, her hair stringy. Perhaps she had been a refugee, or perhaps even a slave. She had not always been noble. No matter what she was capable of looking like now, there was no possible way to beautify that young woman which she had been.

Taking some comfort in the pity she was able to direct toward the woman, Visanna turned away.

She moved through the crowd until she came to seven people surrounding a Ghost Pool, standing with their hands joined. The group peered into the liquid, watching the images created by their conjoined imaginations.

From above they must look like some strange flower, Visanna thought. There are the seven of them forming a ring; behind them are the faces of their past; at their center

17

is the rippling pool.

Within the waters Visanna saw an image of a castle carved from the solid rock of a mountainside, its towers and chambers clinging to sheer cliff faces. A network of ledges and carved staircases led away from the castle like a spider web. A bloodied, armored warrior with a broadsword stood perched on one of the narrow staircases facing down a group of scaly ape-like creatures. Some of the creatures carried stone spikes as weapons.

Visanna looked at the line of misty faces (nearly seventy of them!) behind General Cho. The progression of his faces showed clear demarcations. For periods of years there was a steady march of graceful aging, but three times in his life he had undergone drastic changes, seeming to age decades in a matter of a few years.

Each time his face would rapidly lose some of its color, some of its force of expression. Some process localized in those years had leeched away great parts of his life.

Visanna, as unobtrusively as possible, counted the faces behind the General. She could see that the abrupt changes in the man had occurred ten years ago, twenty-five years ago, and sixty years ago. So it had been the major wars which, even though they had failed to kill the man, had beaten him down. If she looked far enough back, Visanna could see that Cho had been a normal enough child, but had grown up during the decade of the (oddly misnamed) Third Great War. During those years his face had the hollow cheeks and slack skin of a starving child; his eyes the lusterless stare of one who had had to come to terms with violent death far too early and far too often.

Her surreptitious examination of the General's past was broken by the playing of "Ruffles and Flourishes" by the savant musicians. All heads turned to the ballroom entrance.

The Duchess, glowing, stood by the portal. She seemed to drink in the attention of the crowd as a plant, shaded for far too long, would drink in the light of the sun.

A figure appeared.

Some members of the crowd muttered among themselves; a few gasped.

Visanna's heartbeat quickened. She couldn't believe what she was seeing.

All around her people whispered as the uniform and insignia of the figure was recognized.

"So soon? I thought the reparations talks were still going on . . . ."

"How he must feel, here among his enemies! Do you think he feels shame because they lost the war?"

"Is that what one looks like? I would have thought they'd be like some monsters or something . . . ."

At yet none of the people around Visanna dared to even speak of the strangest aspect of the man who now entered the room.

A butler stood at the entrance and called to the hall, "The honored Ambassador from the Kingdom of Chauren."

Visanna couldn't pull her eyes away from the man who nodded and descended the entrance steps, erect with pride but not foolish pride, pacing his stride with neither trepidation nor foolhardiness. And yet Visanna's fascination with the man had nothing to do with the political overtones of his presence.

Visanna could see his current face clearly enough, the face of a middle-aged man, with neatly-trimmed goatee and moustache, skin more tan and leathery than a typical Kavonian, his eyes dark and intense.

And behind him were no faces, absolutely no traces at all of the people he had formerly been. But in front of him

— *in front of him* — were pale, translucent images of the people he would someday be!

Yes, he and he alone, of all the people Visanna had seen in her entire life, possessed images of his own future selves, but that fact alone was not what disturbed Visanna so. What was most unsettling was the fact that the future selves were so few in number.

Surely the Ambassador realized that. Certainly he was aware of the yearly selves which stood before him, growing steadily greyer, steadily more wrinkled, steadily less lustrous of eye, and then, abruptly, five, six, only seven years into the future! — ceasing to exist.

Visanna felt as if the implications of this were closing in over her like the opaque waters of a flood. How did this odd foreigner see himself? Did he conceive of his life as not a culmination of the forces and events of the past, but as an odd and purposeful movement toward a future state of being?

And then the Ambassador was before her, being tugged by the Duchess Harrian.

The faces drifted before her, the face of the Ambassador in the last year of his life closest to her eyes, transparent and mist-like, and behind it another and another and another, back seven years to the current, living-flesh Ambassador, his thinking, living self relegated to a spatial position like that of a ghost whose time is past . . . .

Visanna broke from the grasp of the Duchess, and pushed past the Ambassador from the vanquished land.

She pushed through the crowd, the faces of the living and the faces of those selves they had been looming before her like thick stalks of wheat.

The savant musicians threatened their instruments into a stately and complex melody.

Visanna pushed her way into the entrance hall. An ornate, gilt-framed mirror hung on one wall of the elaborate chamber.

Beneath the surface of the music, a clock groaned into life, and, unnoticed by all except Visanna, struck the hour of midnight.

Visanna looked into the mirror. Within the glass was her face, looking back at her. It was the face which was so familiar from this past year, but as she watched, the features fell away, and took their place directly behind her head, insinuating their way into position before all of the previous years' worth of faces.

And the new face appeared before her, and the mirror — the unforgiving, disinterested mirror! — showed her the new features, the eyes less lustrous, the cheeks sallow, the eyes and mouth more deeply textured with wrinkles, another year's worth of beauty squeezed away by time.

The Duchess in the distance stole glances at her; Artran reached out to place a gentle hand on her shoulders; the servants looked away, afraid to be caught noticing someone of Visanna's class feeling something.

No one acknowledged the radically new face, down which tears were streaming.

THAT NIGHT, IN THEIR BED in the marriage chamber, Artran reached for Visanna. Pliant and calm, she came to him, and responded to him. Moonlight made it easy for her to see over Artran's shoulder as he was over her, and although it was taboo for her to do so, she opened her eyes and looked at the series of faces which looked down at her. The light shone through them. Somewhere back there, somewhere in the past, there might have been an Artran which Visanna could have loved. If so, she couldn't see the face, couldn't catch its attention, couldn't make contact with its eyes as all his faces seemed to long for this one ghostly moment of pleasure from their future.

Much later, in the deepness of the night, Artran slept, breathing steadily and slowly. Visanna lay awake beside him. After lying still and listening to him for nearly an hour, she carefully slipped from between the bedclothes. She pulled on a sheer night-dress, and softly padded up the stone stairs into her private chamber.

The full-length mirror stood in the center of the room. Visanna avoided it as if it were an intruder, an unwelcome guest.

Moonlight shone through her open window. She felt herself drawn to the outside. She drifted across the room, and leaned out to look at the great stretch of village, farm, and forest, and the distant mists of the Meisterilein Mountains.

Below her the surface of the reflecting pool rippled with the slight breeze. Visanna wished to look away before the pool quieted and was ready to show her a reflection. She wished that she could never see herself again, but could instead look as far as possible into the world, to see nothing but new things for the rest of her life.

And deeper than that desire was a vague suspicion she had that if she looked into the pool on *this* night, in *this* light, fired by the feelings that she had now, she would see that she had changed to the same type of faced person as had been the Chaurenian Ambassador; that she would now be a person who was not building on a series of past selves but a person advancing slowly on some future self. Furthermore, she felt a quiet yet steady dread that she would see only a small number of these future selves, and that, like the Chaurenian Ambassador, she would see proof of an

22

impending death a few short years away.

And the breeze died.

And the rippling of the water ceased.

And Visanna, in spite of herself, glanced into the still waters of the pool. She gasped, her heart sank, and she had to clutch at the stone edges of the window frame as she realized exactly what she was seeing.

Just as she had feared, there were no faces behind her. There were faces before her, each one steadily older and less beautiful and more alien to her, representing a future year of her life. What she had not considered, and what she now saw, and what filled her with deepest sadness, was not the fact that there were so few, but the fact that there were so, so many.

Steve Rasnic Tem
The Troll on 23rd Avenue

This isn't me, he told the dark,
damp sheets knotted into rope,
an escape ladder to nowhere
coiled about his huge shape.
This isn't me.

The mirror said, "This is the boy
and now the man, your sad face
and friendless, dreadful flesh.
This old monster haunts you,
and you refuse to see."

Fierce and mad in his burrow,
he went out to commit havoc,
returned at dawn, then down
with rat and roach
into his cellar to weep.

The rat said, "He was kind,
gave me food. But I can't stand
those tears. Life is pain.
Be a rat or be a man."
The roach, indifferent, ate.

The bird said, "He shambled.
He was a shambler. That's how
I knew him best: the beast
who danced with passion,
though he hated the song."

His ears and nose grew faster
than all the rest combined.
Surrounded by hair, his face
lost its way to vagueness
and all hope of a kiss.

He never stole small children;
he was the one they terrified.
If one cursed him he would break.
Magical, malignant, powerful, yet
naked sunlight turned him stone.

He had no place for his tail.
He was brutish and did not eat well.
But he did eat plenty, the poison
of human food, killing himself
with what he did best.

They thought him rich
when he had nothing,
but dreams of traveling the wind.

Cherie Priest
The Immigrant

I.

*F*OUND AMONG THE PAPERS *of Ryder Neal, on the day
after his funeral, July 30, 1996, Jonesboro, Tennessee.*

"Venez m'aider," he said.

With a jaw like that, so long and underbitten like a
boxer dog, you wouldn't have thought he could speak at all.
His face wasn't made for talking, but he forced the words
out. He said it again, quiet-like.

"Venez m'aider."

I knew what it meant. I didn't know ten words of
French total, but I knew those last two, pushed together
with an apostrophe, if you wrote them out.

He looked like a cross between a lizard and a cat, or he
did when he was sitting, anyway. When he stood and
unfolded himself, he was the size of a pillow, maybe — but
so slender, with bones so thin they must have been fragile.
Something about the way he held that one wing back . . .
something about his crouch, all submissive — like a dog or
a kid afraid of being hit — it made me think he was a
brittle little thing.

He had my attention, and he knew it. I don't know why
I thought of him automatically as a 'he,' but it must have
been that voice. It could've been a boy's voice, if that boy
were very tired, and maybe sick.

We stared at each other for a minute.

He looked at me through half-closed eyes, and he
probably figured the worst. I was a mess, and I looked
mean. It'd been less than a month since Normandy. I'd been

26

lucky enough to make it past the beach, then they sent us down through France, which wasn't half so bad — once you got past that initial reception. As soon as we got into Paris they sent me and a few others to dislodge the last of the Germans — the ones who hadn't got the message yet that Paris had been liberated. Most of them had run out ahead of us, but there were a few here and there digging in and holding out.

I thought I'd heard something, you know how it is — down a dark alley, in a beat-up part of the city. Don't want to look. Don't want to check. Don't want to go. Seen enough already.

But orders are orders, so you do it anyhow.

I told myself it was a few stray bricks, falling from an unlucky wall or a shell-battered house. I knew the Krauts hadn't been too hard on the city, not compared to other places. But there were beat-up spots here and there, and I'd found one. I just hoped the spot was unoccupied. That was the trick.

Heaven heard half of that prayer, I guess, which is fitting since it was the shot-open basement of a fancy church. A door like a storm cellar's hatch had been broken. It swung free and loose from its hinge. Stairs led down into the dark, and I followed them with my gun drawn and pointed, because that's how you survive going into dark places that have unexplained noises in them.

Down at the bottom of the stairs, in a room with a few prayer candles for light, I found a dead priest. He'd been there long enough to be good and stiff, but not long enough to smell ripe. I got a whiff of blood, though — lots of blood. I stepped in it, too. I slipped a tiny bit before catching myself, and before catching a glimpse of *him*.

He was curled beneath a table, behind the priest. At first I thought he'd killed the prostrate man in the cassock, so at first I jerked the gun up and pointed it hard at the pair of eyes I saw down close to the floor.

That's when he spoke.

You can shoot a scary-looking dog, if it comes down to it. You can shoot a vicious-looking animal, even if it's not threatening you yet. There's a trigger in your head, and it tells you when there's danger, even before you've got all your information.

Even though he was less than half my size, and hiding, and not making any threatening gestures, some primal urge was just yanking at that mental trigger . . . until he breathed that plea. *"M'aider."*

You can't shoot something so strange when it talks to you like that. Not out of hand. Not if it asks for help.

Besides, even at a dozen paces I could see that the priest had been shot.

When I looked at the thing's hands — they weren't really hands, but close enough — I was pretty sure they couldn't have held a gun. They couldn't have pulled a trigger. Not easily. Not deliberately, with those webs and blunt, thumb-thick claws.

I lowered the tip of the rifle. He hadn't hurt anybody, and he was doing his best to indicate that he wouldn't hurt me.

"What are you?" I asked. His forehead wrinkled just like a man's — just like he was listening, and trying to understand. "Jesus Christ, what the hell are you?"

Jesus' name he knew. He nodded, because I guess he misunderstood. I remembered then that we were underneath a church. Those crazy hands of his came together to make a prayer with a steeple point.

"Oui," he said, and unclasped his hands to gesture at the candles. Behind them, blotted with shadows, a statue of Mary leaned against a wall.

"Oui." I said it back, because it was one other word I knew, and hell — what do you say to something like that?

To something like *him*?

With a pained shuffle and lurch, he turned his side to face me. My first impression had been right. Something was wrong with his wing. When the flickering light hit it directly I saw that it was bent at a bad angle, probably broken — but not in a way where any bones were poking through, so it could've been worse.

He was showing me he was harmless. He was showing me he needed help, in case I didn't catch the French.

I put the gun down slow. I put my hands out in front of me, and I sort of hunkered down, tiptoeing towards him. I'd had enough of people wanting to hurt me in the last few months, so if he didn't want to hurt me, I didn't want to hurt him. I didn't know what he was, but if he wasn't a Kraut and he was in trouble, then I didn't mind helping him if I could.

He let me approach, and even held out the wing for me to look. I touched it as gently as I could, feeling my way along it. His skin was smooth and pretty gold-red. Covered with scales, it looked like it ought to feel slimy, but it was dry and soft — like the tight, expensive gloves the French girls wore.

"Ah," he grunted when I hit a swollen spot. I thought he was objecting, but he didn't pull away. He made the noise again, and finished the question. "American?" The word sounded funny in his mouth, with the accents in the wrong place and the vowels laid out flat.

"Yeah, that's right. American. That's me. Let me see it. Let me help."

And he did. It's not like I was a medic or anything, because I wasn't; but even if I had been, I don't think there was a doctor in the corps who could've splinted that crazy wing.

Under the candles, and under some mortar debris on the table, there was a cloth. I pulled it off and shook it, flapping it open like my mother used to spread out sheets on the bed. I dropped it down over him like a cloak, or a blanket.

When I picked him up, he was as light as a child.

II.

THE TRICK WAS GETTING HIM HOME, obviously. It doesn't bear much of a dry retelling, so suffice it to say, I had to ship him back with me as freight. I set him up as best I could. It turned out, he would eat almost anything edible and he didn't much care what it was. It took some doing, but I got him put on my own transport home so I could keep an eye on him. This also made it easier to slip him better food, once in awhile; though truth to tell, there were times I thought about trading with him for the good French dog chow I'd scored for him.

My sergeant knew what was going on, or he thought he did. He thought I was sneaking a dog back, maybe. It happened every now and again, and he was good enough to look the other way. He said if I got caught with contraband on board, he didn't know anything about it and it was nobody's problem but mine.

So I kept it my problem. I kept sneaking downstairs into the cargo hold with a bag of dog food and sometimes, a covered tin plate of army chow. It wasn't as if I was going to eat it all, anyway. Army cooking at its finest can't hold a candle to what my Alice can do with a stove.

Speaking of Alice, I spent many a night wondering how I was going to explain *him* to her.

How do you start that conversation with your wife? "Hi honey, I'm home. Meet the weird little French dragon I found under a table in a church. His name is Pierre, I think. That's what I think he said. That's what I started calling him, anyway."

I started teaching him English, too. He picked it up a whole lot better and a whole lot faster than I ever caught on to French. By the time I got him back to east Tennessee, we could manage a fair outline of a conversation.

Those first attempts at talking sounded like a man teaching a dog how to sit and speak, I imagine. I didn't mean it that way. I wasn't trying to treat him like he was dumb. But he was small and quiet, and four-legged plus a pair of wings. He wasn't a dog, and he wasn't a child — but he was my charge. And if I was going to get him home safe, he needed to know how to be quiet on cue.

Like I said, he was a quick study.

III.

HOME WAS A PARCEL OF LAND in the Appalachians, just a few miles away from where Davy Crockett was born. The nearest town was Jonesboro, and the nearest town of any size was Johnson City. I tell you that just to give you some frame of reference, because otherwise you wouldn't really know how far out into the sticks we were.

That's one reason I thought it might be safe to bring Pierre home. There was no one around to see him and worry — not for miles. Our nearest neighbors made their living selling homemade alcohol and hiding it from Uncle Sam, so I figured the odds weren't too good they'd run to the police even if they saw anything strange.

Alice was my only worry.

I'd married a farm girl. She could grow or butcher most of her own food, or bottle-feed a lamb if it came to that. She was one of the most competent and practical women I ever knew.

So I decided to trust her, and trust that level-headed steadiness. A friend of mine helped unload the pick-up truck with my duffel bag, a few presents from Europe, and that big damn crate with the suspicious-looking holes in the top.

Pierre was as silent as luggage. We deposited him in the barn, in a quiet back stall away from the horses.

It took me awhile to get rid of Andy, who wanted a round of beers and war stories before he'd go on his way; but once he was gone I took Alice by the hand and led her back out to the barn.

"I've got something to show you," I told her. "I found him in Paris — "

"Him?" She frowned at me, and at the crate. "Dear God Almighty, don't tell me you've left something alive in there?"

"He's — yeah. He's alive. But I couldn't just send him like a puppy or anything, Alice. He's different. He's *real* different. And he's hurt, but not too bad." I took a crowbar and pried at the lid. "He needs a place to rest up and heal."

The lid came up, and I pulled down the panel that hid Pierre, exposing him to the dim, barn-filtered light . . . and to Alice, who covered her mouth with her hands.

"Jesus," she said.

Pierre was crouched with his face in a corner. He turned slowly and blinked at the light, and at my wife. "He's just like one of us, baby, and hurt by the Nazis. I couldn't leave him there."

She sank to a low squat, in order to meet him on eye level. "It's his wing, isn't it? It's broken."

"Broken," he whispered back. He knew that word, so he knew to agree.

"He talks." It wasn't a question. She never asked stupid questions. "Jesus, Lord. What is he?"

He got the gist, and he answered, more or less. "Pierre," he said, patting his chest and looking at Alice with a fresh sort of hope, or optimism.

"Pierre. Dammit Ryder, you weren't going to keep him

32

out here in the barn were you?"

I looked to the dragon, like he would answer for me, or for himself. "I was going to put him, I figured, wherever he wanted to go. I couldn't see talking Andy into helping me carry the crate up to the guest room, though. He'd have wanted to see what was inside, and you're the first person I've tried to show this fellow to."

"Well all right then. Pierre. Sweetheart, let me take a look at that. Let me see what we can do. That's a nice name, Pierre. Who gave you that name? Not Ryder, I don't bet."

"The priest," he murmured. "He said I hatched from a stone."

IV.

HE STAYED INSIDE WITH US, for a few weeks. We put him in the guest bedroom, where Alice's mother and father stayed when they came to visit, before they died. He didn't much care for the bed, and was happier sleeping under it. That was okay with us. It made him easier to hide during the occasional, unexpected, uninvited welcome-home visitor.

We must've gotten fifteen casseroles that first month after I came back. It was sweet of everyone — it was nice to feel appreciated and all — but when you've got a secret as strange as Pierre, you'd just as soon have the world leave you alone.

When we had the place to ourselves, Pierre roamed freely. We came to think of him as a really smart kid; he was about the size of a first or second grader, and he had that same kind of permanent curiosity about him. He touched everything, but he never broke anything. He asked a lot of questions, always in that soft-spoken voice that never did lose the pretty Paris lilt that Alice liked so much to hear.

He used to talk to me and Alice over breakfast, when my wife would make eggs, bacon, and grits for all three of us. I couldn't believe how much he could eat in one sitting, but he was a growing boy.

He wasn't sure how old he was, but he thought he must be ten or eleven. Just a youngster. For as long as he could remember, he'd lived at the church with Jean, the priest who had died — the priest had been shot after an argument. A German soldier had gotten a peek at Pierre, and he'd cornered the priest downstairs.

"He told Jean, 'You must give me the monster that sleeps behind the altar.' But Jean said no. They argued, and I was afraid."

"Of course you were, baby," Alice cooed. "Anybody would have been."

"Jean was not. Jean locked me in the place where people went to say their sins. He would not open the door, and he would not tell the soldier where I was. That's why he died."

"So what were you doing in the basement, then?" I asked. There was no confessional down there that I had seen.

"I followed him there, once I pushed my way out. Jean had lived, for a little while. Down underneath, it was dark and quiet. But then there was a big noise, and the wall fell. I tried to cover him. That's how I hurt myself. I knew he died. But I did not know where else to go. Then you came."

"Mmm." Alice shook her head and put another load of fried eggs onto his plate. It's a southern thing, I guess — the desire to feed people when you don't know how else to comfort them. "Bless your heart."

He didn't use a knife or fork, but we forgave him. It looked awkward when he tried, so he ate instead with his not-quite-hands. He was fussy and delicate with his food. It never seemed rude at all. It was like watching someone from another country, with manners that were every bit as good as yours, but different.

This was a reminder, though — every mealtime — that he was not like us. That he was something else. He was something different.

You don't want to talk about a rational creature as an animal, but he was clearly not a person, either. He was thoughtful, and helpful. The horses liked him, and he liked them; he had a general affinity for living things, which was nice. As he healed, he spent more and more time outside . . . until he announced that he preferred the barn after all.

By then his wings were strong enough to hold him.

The first time I saw him fly it made my chest hurt, it was so weird and so pretty. You see big birds, sometimes. Even the biggest, ugliest buzzards look like angels in the air. It doesn't jive in a person's head, how something so heavy and strong can flap and soar like that.

That's how Pierre looked, too. A small coppery angel, he flapped his way around the farm. In the sun, he was a thing of myth, not monster. He was a thing of beauty — one of God's own creatures, I'd swear it.

The dead French priest knew it. He must have. Me and Alice weren't brought up papists; but same as most folks we knew, we were Christians. And we're all looking up to the same sky — at the same God. At the same birds. At Pierre.

All of us have the same questions and requests when we close our eyes and bow our heads.

V.

ALICE TAUGHT HIM HIS ABCs, and with a lot of effort, Pierre could write. It took years before his penmanship was good enough to read, but once it did, he wrote a lot. He used to ask for paper and pens. He liked the big sheets — the kinds that artists use, they come in pads. I bought them for him in town. He liked big pencils, too. The thin ones broke in his hand, as he got bigger and stronger.

He did get bigger, too. A lot bigger. When he was a little fellow, he used to fly around during the day, happy as a pig in mud. But by the time he quit growing (or grew so slow that we didn't notice anymore), he was the size of a good working horse.

It got to where he only flew at night, so he didn't scare people. He was a thoughtful thing. He never wanted to bother anyone. Never wanted to make any trouble.

But people did see him, once in awhile. Stories got out and around, as stories tend to do. The first stories were predictably hysterical — there's a monster in the woods outside Jonesboro! There's a dragon in the forest, eating livestock and burning barns! Well, Pierre enjoyed a good steak as much as anybody, but he didn't kill his own that I ever knew of. And if he could start a fire without a box of matches, I never saw him do it.

After awhile, though, the stories changed in timbre and tone.

After awhile, there were stories about strange angels. Lost kids were led back to town by a bright-winged creature that flew low enough to follow. Campers trapped in the snow would awaken to find themselves dug out, with paths leading off in the right direction. The paths would be stamped down with the most extraordinary footprints you ever saw, but they were always true and safe to follow. Missing sheep were returned unharmed to their pens.

One time, one of our moonshining neighbors had a still that went bust. A fire broke out and made its way to the house they had, and it was just a wood clapboard thing so it went right up in smoke. On the second floor there was a 3-year-old girl, and everyone knew for sure she was dead to rights.

While the fire still burned, they found that girl behind

the house. She was standing in her nightgown, bare feet in the grass. She was looking up at the sky, and she was smiling.

Years later, when that girl was in third grade, she was told to write a polite thank you note for a school project. Her mother brought the note to us because she thought it was cute, and because the kid insisted. It was written on that big-ruled paper, hardly thicker than tissue. It was addressed "to the red stone dragon, at Ryder Neal's place."

We showed it to Pierre and he nodded solemnly. He wrote her a short letter in reply, and asked that we deliver it. Their little correspondence went on that way for years; and in time, a few of the other school kids started leaving notes for him too. They put them out in the barn, in the clean stall back behind the horses. They left letters, and drawings, and chocolates there as if it were a shrine.

Pierre didn't mind if the kids' parents thought we wrote his responses.

It didn't matter to us, either, that the world thought we were participating in some cutesy joke, like Santa Claus or the Tooth Fairy. It could be our secret, though some of the little ones knew better.

And those little ones, when they grew up and had little ones of their own, they passed the stories down and along. Maybe now there are a dozen people these days who know the truth. There's no way to say. Everybody talks about our dragon with a wink in one eye and a sparkle in the other.

Alice and I never did have any kids of our own, but we were never lonely for them, and all of these years, we have counted ourselves blessed.

Sheree Renée Thomas
Once

Once
we said thunder
was Old Sista Sky
                picking out her naps
    untangling the knots
in her kitchen
lightning was Old Sista
                firing up her hot comb
    the mist   great hiss
of iron

And rain, sweet rain
Old Scratch heavy hands
                parting Sista stubborn hair
        'cuz everybody know
Old Sista tenderheaded
                cry like she ain't got
        no natural
sense

She want them fancy braids
twisting lovely in shiny rows
hair so pretty, reverse the way
Sweet River flow, Old Sista
tenderheaded but she vain
can't sit still, can't take the pain
Old Sista yelp, Old Sista holla
make Scratch so mad
he comb her harder

Now
water all up to our knees
now, water all 'round our neck
we don't welcome Old Sista tears no more
we ask the heavy hands to be still
just grease her scalp, we say
let Old Sista Sky head alone
bump her edges if you must
can't you braid no cornrows
without all that fuss?

Now, Old Scratch slick
Old Scratch mean
but he still didn't expect
this much vex

Before he dig teeth
in tender scalp
Old Sista jump up
with a shout
Before he could stomp, before he could moan
Old Sista don' up and snatch the devil comb
she beat Scratch above, beat Scratch below
they fought so long, they forgot the damn stove
hot comb burnin', hair grease smokin'
the heat turnt up too high
great blast of fire is how Sun got to Sky

So when you see the rain fallin'
but light shining bright
Remember the night
Old Scratch got whooped
by Old Sista Sky

Sheree Renée Thomas

untitled Old Scratch poem, featuring River

Old Scratch, soul taker
womb breaker, shapeshifter
forever playin', turnin'
his bitter tongue to sweet balm
his hailstorms to soft Wind
strokin' backs like he
know something 'bout
gentle

Breeze-breezin' joy
To all he touch
But you can't trust
the wind, 'cause wind
play too damn much

Old Scratch think
He a mac from way, way back,
Player from the old time, the Time
Before, choosing up on a fly girl
Like me. He forget my daddy
name me River, sweetness
from God second day, can't be
Breeze-breezin' up on me
'cause daddy didn't raise
no fool

Old Scratch think he something
Hum humming softly, wine
and sultry whispers strokin'
my bellyskin, palm palmin'
over my face and shoulders
shimmer me wet
like I don't know he sang
that same tired song to Old Sista Sky
he ought to know
I am outside to no one
afterthought to none
I let his sugar lies
drop like old stones
in the bottom of the sea
and swing my big hips
on by, on by

Catherynne M. Valente
Temnaya and the House of Books

ONCE UPON A TIME, in a land of mist and pines far away from this one, across thrice nine kingdoms, a young couple lived in a modest house on the edge of a forest. It was a pleasant place, with a red roof and peonies growing like a carpet of violet and gold leading up to the rounded door. They were very happy, and spent their days among boiling water and the thick slap of axe against wood. Meat glistened in their one iron pot; cakes steamed on the hewn hawthorn of their windowsill. The sun was silver in the morning, and red at dusk.

They were very happy, except that they did not have a child.

They prayed and prayed, and the wife ate green and unripe fruits cut with a copper knife from the furthest tree in the forest, under the light of the waning moon. She cut up her beloved peonies into an ugly paste, and wept as she swallowed the once-velvet blossoms. She took brisk walks at twilight, in order to make her womb placid as clouds, but she never conceived.

FINALLY, THEY DECIDED that it was not the will of God that they should have a child of their own.

ONE EVENING IN LATE SUMMER, the young wife was sitting by her window, and playing a sweet, sad song on her little wooden harpsichord, which was painted delicately with scenes of contented milkmaids and docile cows chewing grass of threaded jade. It was the young wife's only fine thing, a gift from her own mother, when she was a girl and had not yet thought of how to solder pots with her own hands. As she played a delicate minuet, full of undulating scales like rivers tumbling downhill, she looked out into the night, so full of stars, and wished that she could have a daughter with hair as black as the sky before dawn, skin as white as the snow which had not yet come, and a voice as sweet as her own rippling song.

Just then, she struck a false note in her minuet, and though she slept that night thinking nothing of it, not long after, she gave birth to a girl with hair as black as the sky before dawn, skin as white as snow which had not yet fallen, and a little cry like a lonely bird singing in the wood. She looked again into the frosted corners of the night, and with the warm child at her breast, called her one and only daughter Temnaya.

Now, the young mother did not die, as so many mothers in tales will, but the husband, who had never been enamored of the sound of axe biting into wood, and was not overfond of the same mute meat in the same old pot night after night, tired of her and left their pleasant house with his daughter tied onto his back like a little satchel before the child had spoken her first word.

Time passed, and at length he married a younger woman, who was unlike his first wife in every way. And he took Temnaya from the land of mist and quiet woods and into the grand house of this new woman, who did not play the harpsichord at all.

NOW, IT HAPPENED that this stepmother had in her possession a magic mirror, polished to gleaming and rimmed in carved walnut, which she kept hidden in the smallest room of her many-gabled house. It was her prize and her pride, but since she had married the strange, soft-spoken man who would not, under any circumstances, chop wood for the fire, it had become her secret, and her shame.

Each day she would uncover the magic mirror and in it

she would see, not her own unlined face, but the image of the first wife, unlike her in every way. The stepmother's hair was the color of straw, and she kept it short, styled in the latest fashion. The first wife had hair the color of the sky before dawn, just like her daughter's, and it was very long and wild. The stepmother loved fine clothes and jewels; the first wife dressed in tweed and wool. The stepmother did not like books, she kept only a few scattered about the house, to keep up appearances — and yet the mirror always showed the first wife reading. The second wife had practiced her smile in this very mirror as a child, until it was fastened to her face as securely as a window in a wall, but the first wife's reflection never smiled, and her beauty was hard and cruel and old, though not less, never less than the carefully drawn lines of the new woman's face.

Yet they both had the same eyes, blue as chips of ice struck from a glacier. Each day the stepmother would scowl at this image and ask a question learned from all the old stories:

> *Mirror, mirror, on the wall,*
> *who is the fairest of them all?*

And the image would shimmer to show the stepmother herself, as she knew herself to be. Satisfied, she would cover her mirror and go into her house.

Now, the stepmother hated the little girl her husband had brought with him. She did not herself understand why, only that those dark, muddy features and frightened, fluttering fingers were grotesque to her, a horror masquerading as a child. She bore her own children as quickly as possible, hoping that he would forget about the daughter with hair as black as the sky before dawn and a voice like a lonely bird singing in the wood. Her children were as beautiful as her arts could make them, with hair of gold and her own ice-blue eyes — yet she bore only sons, and so the husband did not forget his only daughter, and the stepmother's anger grew.

As Temnaya grew, she began to look more and more like her mother. Her hair grew long and wild, her snowy skin had no blemish, even when streaked with clay from days spent frog-hunting in hidden swamps — and the girl always found the swamps, no matter how fine their gardens and grounds. Her reedy voice became low and sweet. She dressed in wool and secreted books away beneath her bed, and she played the harpsichord very well when the music-masters visited the village. The stepmother's hatred of the girl knew no bounds, she scolded her constantly for infractions of etiquette and dress, and made her clean the enormous house three times a day.

ONE MORNING, THE STEPMOTHER looked into her mirror, into the face of the first wife, and her loathing bubbled up afresh.

> *Mirror, mirror, on the wall,*
> *who is the fairest of them all?*

The image shimmered, but instead of the stepmother's own face, she saw the swamp-soaked face of Temnaya sitting at the edge of a scummy green pond, with hair as black as the sky before dawn, reading a red book and chewing the stem of a cattail. The stepmother, her face purpled with rage, resolved to drive the child from her house.

First, she enticed the girl into the wood, with kisses and new ribbons for presents, and all the artifice of affection, whose manufacture is a witch's greatest tool. She packed them a picnic, and Temnaya was very happy to go, for she hardly remembered her own mother, and loved her step-mother very much. But when they had arrived in the

45

deepest, darkest part of the wood, the stepmother beat the child with her fists until her beautiful, snow-white skin was purple and black with bruises, and blood trickled from her eyes like tears. Temnaya did not struggle, but waited for it to be over. Her stepmother shut her eyes while she did it, and would not look at the broken cheekbones or shattered teeth, for her heart was stretched on hooks between her desire to have the child gone and her desire to think herself a good and virtuous woman.

In the end, the stepmother left her child to die alone in the deepest part of the wood, and returned to her grand, many-gabled house, telling her husband that little Temnaya was playing in the forest and would not be home for supper.

IN THE LONG SHADOWS of the forest, surrounded by gnarled roots and sound-swallowing pine needles, Temnaya was very afraid. To cheer herself she sang a little song, and her sweet voice filled the wood like that of a lonely bird. When she had finished her song, she was not so afraid, but her face hurt terribly.

Suddenly, another little song filled the trees, and she spied a small, brown bird. It chirruped, repeating her song, and hopping away through the wood. The girl followed the bird through the darkness and very soon found herself at home, just as her stepmother and the other children were finishing their supper. The stepmother was very angry, but she smiled sweetly for her husband and asked her step-daughter where she had gotten such terrible bruises. Temnaya lied very bravely. She looked at her stepmother with love and sorrow, and slowly, through her ruined mouth, said, "Mother mine, I fell into a little brook and cut my face on rocks under the swift water. I am sorry; I am clumsy, as you well know."

The father was satisfied, and the little girl went away to bed without a word.

Certain, at least, that with such wounds, the little girl could not now be as fair as she, the stepmother asked her mirror again the next morning, her voice full of confidence:

> *Mirror, mirror, on the wall,*
> *who is the fairest of them all?*

The image of the first wife shimmered and in its place was Temnaya, huddled by her scummy green pond, arms wrapped around thin, bent knees, with hair as black as the sky before dawn, her poor face swollen with yellowing weals, reading her little book.

The stepmother was speechless with fury.

This time, she went to her husband and told him that his daughter was a very wicked little girl, and that she must be punished. He loved his second wife, and her beauty was so great that he was dazzled when she stood between him and his child, and he saw Temnaya through her stepmother as through a fire, her little body distorted by waves of heat and light. He agreed that his daughter must be a sneaky, ugly, fat little child--after all, her mother had been so tiresome, with her endless meat-stews, and daughters must take after their mothers—it is the natural order of things. And so, the stepmother did not allow the girl to eat for many days, hoping that she would fall into a swoon and perish. The father was often away, and did not notice anything amiss, and through the fire saw only that Temnaya was a bit quieter and thinner than usual, which could only be to the good.

Of course, the child was very hungry. But she knew that she had done something wrong, though she could not think what, and did not complain. She read her books in secret and did not come out of her room, and every time she heard her stepmother's footsteps her heart seized in terror, terror and hope. On the seventh day without food, she had

47

finished the few books she was allowed to keep for herself, and to pass the time, she sang a little song, her voice filling the room like that of a lonely bird in a wood. When she had finished the song, a little brown bird fluttered onto her windowsill with a hunk of bread in its beak, as thick and brown as its own feathers. The bread was so large it was hard to believe the bird could carry it, but the little girl took it gratefully. Each day she sang her song and the bird brought her scraps of food, so that she did not fall into a swoon, and soon began to grow more beautiful than ever, as her face healed and her snow-white skin shone out under the last of her bruises.

Finally, the stepmother gave up. Still, she was sure that the little girl, with her wild hair, her muddy face, and her ugly clothes, must have lost her beauty as she starved. And so, once again, she uncovered her mirror, and once again, she was confronted by the image of the first wife. She grimaced as though she had eaten unripe fruit.

> *Mirror, mirror, on the wall,*
> *who is the fairest of them all?*

And the image shimmered to show the child with hair as black as the sky before dawn, playing at the music-master's harpsichord, with dirt under her perfect fingernails. The stepmother screamed her hate into the glass — but she seized upon a plan.

That evening, she went to her husband and said, "We have our own children, with hair of gold and ice-blue eyes. Let the girl go to her mother, and we will be rid of her. Daughters should be with their mothers — it is the natural order of things. It would be a kindness."

At long last, the father agreed, and packed a little satchel for his daughter. Temnaya's dark eyes were full of tears, for she loved her father, and her brothers, and most especially her stepmother, whom she thought in her heart to be the fairest woman in the world. The stepmother, with her practiced smile thrown open as a window sash in summer, sent the child into the wood, to find the house of her mother.

"It is only a little way into the wood, my pet," she said, and wrapped Temnaya in an honest and gleeful embrace. She waved good-bye, like a mother.

With the girl with skin as white as snow not-yet-fallen gone, the stepmother was sure she would be happy. And indeed, soon after that, she bore a daughter with hair of gold and eyes blue as chips of ice struck from a glacier. She held the child in her arms and said:

"I will make this girl unlike his first daughter in every way. Her hair will always be silky and curled, she will wear the finest clothes and jewels, and she will never read a book or play in a swamp. I will love her best of all things in the world, and one day, when I am past my youth, she will be as fair as I."

THIS TIME, THE LITTLE GIRL was not afraid of the forest, for she knew her little brown birds would come if they were needed. Though in her heart she was sad, and missed her brothers, thinking often as she wandered of how they wrestled like young lions, she walked with her head high, and hoped that her real mother would love her.

The wood was all silver and red with autumn, and leaves blew with crackle and rasp against her bare calves. The thin light was slanted, and strange.

It was longer than her stepmother had said, and a full day and night passed before she began to see a little footpath in the forest, which led up a small hill to a most extraordinary house. It was made entirely of books, from door to chimney. Large books and small books, thick books and thin books, books with leather bindings and books with dog-eared pages. The walls were spines facing outward, like a well-ordered shelf, hung with long, fluttering rainspout-ribbonmarks the color of new blood, and atop the hut was a red bent-spine roof with shingles of uncut pages. The windows were made of vellum so old you could see through it, and the flower-boxes were filled with little pamphlets growing on slender green stalks. In a long winding carpet before the rounded folio-porch was row after row of violet and gold scrolls, capped with green wax. The door was the largest book the little girl had ever seen, a dictionary even larger than her favorite one at home, and it swung open on its enormous spine, the *K* section pointing inward.

Temnaya took this as a welcome, and walked into the strange house.

A woman sat at a harpsichord piled high with yellowed music, her dark head bent low over the keys. When she looked up, Temnaya was surprised to see that the woman looked just like her, if somewhat older and more worn around the eyes. Her hair was black as the sky after the moon has gone, long and wild, and her skin was like the last snow before spring, but her mouth was cruel, and the girl quailed before her twisted frown, unsure of herself. She twisted her fingers around her hair, as was her habit when she was frightened. The older woman pursed her pale lips and seemed to examine Temnaya with some invisible glass.

"Anyone can tell by looking at you that you've been . . . ruined," the woman said. "He shouldn't have taken you away, now you've been raised by a witch and ruined for the respectable world. The books won't take you now; you stink like swamp and bad women."

Nevertheless, she kissed her daughter's cheek coldly, and gave her a little bowl of leek- and-quarto soup. She told her to stay out of the way, and not to spill any on the books. And so mother and daughter passed many days this way, neither speaking nor touching. Temnaya's mother played very beautifully, without a single false note, and read her books to herself. She read the walls and the stairs, hunched over the railings, her fingers skillfully touching the raised banister-braille; she hunched in the rafters and read the ceiling with spectacles on, she read the lexicon-chairs and the calligraphy of the floorboards. She was like a strange, dark bat, fluttering from page to page, appearing without sound at the side of chapter after chapter. Temnaya watched her sharp-faced mother with awe.

And each evening she went away to another part of the house where it was clear the little girl was not welcome.

As it often happens, curiosity alighted on Temnaya's shoulder like a grackle with needle-claws. One evening the little girl crept behind her mother and followed her up to the attic, to see what it was she did when the sun went down in the sky. She did not mean to be impolite, but the grackle was very insistent, and its voice in her ear was shrill.

She watched from the stairwell as her mother pulled a great oval mirror, polished to gleaming and rimmed in carved walnut from a closet made of two slim blue books of etiquette and stood in front of it, frowning. The image within the silver glass was not her own, but that of Temnaya's stepmother, with her hair of straw and her bright clothing. She was holding the chubby hand of a baby taking its first steps, her emerald skirt brushing against the child's pink ankles, and catching her shock of golden hair in its beadwork.

"No matter what," her mother said quietly, "it only shows me her." Temnaya was startled in her hiding place, and trembled in her pale skin.

> *Mirror, mirror, on the wall,*
> *who is the wisest one of all?*

The image shimmered and showed her beautiful, cruel mother, her wild hair, black as the sky after the moon has

51

gone, flying behind her like torn flags. She smiled ruefully.

"What is more wicked than a stepmother, more wicked than a father? The mantle-manual tells me that this yellow-haired creature and I are connected by you like a child is connected to its womb by an umbilicus. You are our umbilicus, fat and dark and useless — you serve only to stand between two others and drag blood from one to the other. As long as you lie there like a worm between us, my mirror will never show me my own face, only the face of the one woman in the world who is unlike me in every way. I am your mother, and I say that *you ought not to have been born*. It was only an idle wish, nothing more. A silly wish — and all these horrors came. You have brought me nothing but misery, and now you sneak and hide when I have given you the hospitality of my house. I might have loved you, if you had not been such a stupid, mewling little mouse. You are nothing but a wish poorly made, and now we are all caught in it, in your greasy whorls, your bloody knots."

Temnaya started to protest, her dark eyes filling up with tears.

"I was only trying to be good, I'm sorry, I will speak and read and sing and be nothing at all like a mouse — "

But her mother seized her by the wrist and pulled her down the encyclopedia-steps, into the epistle-papered kitchen. She opened a great yawning oven, whose door was the cover of a black Bible. The pages fluttered frantically and caught flame.

"Everything will go back to the way it was," her mother said shrilly, "it will be as if I never grew old, as if I was never alone, as if you never were!"

Temnaya, with her skin as white as snow unfallen and her hair as black as the sky before dawn, opened her red lips and in her terror sang her little song, her voice filling the oven like a lonely bird in a wood — but no small brown birds came. She sang again, and still no comforting feathers

52

beat back the fire. She was alone, and very small in her mother's arms.

They struggled, Temnaya and her mother, who was so much taller and stronger than she. The light in her ice-blue eyes was like lightning slashing through rain. Many times, the little girl grappled with the woman, hoping only to keep her back, begging her to stop. Still, she pulled her daughter closer and closer to the blue-and-orange flames. Temnaya was so close to the terrible furnace that she could see, she could see the licking fire, and realized that they, too, were scraps of rice paper, with verses written in flame still scrawling themselves out, so that they burned even as they rhymed themselves into holocaust.

Finally, Temnaya caught a length of her mother's wild hair, black as the sky after the moon has gone, and pulled hard, tilting her headlong into the oven.

The little girl stared after, hot tears rolling down her face, as her mother burned on a pyre of pages.

FAR OFF, ON THE EDGE OF THE WOOD, the stepmother began to feel hot, and scratched at her skin as though a shower of ash had spattered her. She could not seem to cool herself, no matter how many icy baths she drew, or how many soaked scarves she wrapped around her red and steaming arms. She begged her children to cover her in ice, and this they did, loyally as children will, until the woman was walled up in an old icehouse, her burning skin melting through the ice, which had to be replaced every evening, so that she could sleep. Her mouth only just peeked out through a small hole in the silver ice-blocks, giving orders for the roasting of ducks and potatoes and doling out punishments for dirty feet, and thus she would remain for the rest of her days.

* * *

53

THE NEXT MORNING, Temnaya sat at her mother's harpsichord, and the house was very, very quiet, without even the comforting sound of pages turning in the wind. Off in the distance, a bird sang mournfully which might, if she chose to believe it, be small and sweet and brown.

SHE TOLD HERSELF she would not look in the mirror. She would never look in the mirror. Of course she wouldn't.

TIME PASSED, AND TEMNAYA grew up alone in the house of books. She learned how to sit just so in order to read the ceiling, and her hair grew long, long and wild.

One evening, in late summer, Temnaya was sitting by her vellum-window and playing a sweet, sad minuet on the harpsichord, full of undulating scales like rivers tumbling downhill. Her gaze was lost in the grass-jade patterns graved into the wood, and the dictionary-door wafted lazily against the jam. She looked up and out, into the night, so full of stars, and wished that she could have a little daughter with hair as black as the sky before dawn, skin as white as the snow that would soon come, and a voice as sweet as her own rippling song.

JUST THEN, she struck a false note in her minuet.

JoSelle Vanderhooft
The Tale of the Desert
that Vanished Inside Her

I.

She was only seventeen.

Her face was so mangled, even that was hard to determine.

Then again, a Desert always knows these things. We have to, everything they throw inside us — old tires, smashed glass, enough rusting cars to build a new horizon — yes, we must know. Or we would not understand how to digest.

I touched her legs and hands — five hours dead, at least, and the mess —

who could have thought so much blood could hide inside the heart?

I waited just a little for the light. And then, I moved.

II.

God, oh God.
I shouldn't be — I shouldn't be —
I shouldn't be torn.
I should move, I should breathe I should run, I
*   should cry.*
I should have eyes. I should know. I should hear and
*   feel.*
I shouldn't be here. Not here, not now.
Help me
Help

III.

Even deserts aren't perfect, and sometimes we get it wrong.

This was one of those times, I guess.

Still, I'm a relentless thing. The sun must rise, the sun must fall, and I must eat. Even now, great things stir underneath my skin; a mouth of snakes and lizard teeth. I can't deny them any more than I can overrule the sun, any more than I can overrule the burn inside my coils.

But I can listen. I slide against her sides like rattle snakes and turn my head.

The wind picks up.

It blows my hair against the terror of her face.

Against the gunfire of her belly.

Against the slaughter of her thighs.

Against the ruin of her lips.

Against the tatters of her wedding dress that covers her no better than the air.

IV.

Where is he?
I shouldn't be — I shouldn't be —
I shouldn't be broken.
Not here, and not like this.
    I shouldn't be alone
    He should be here
    Why isn't he?
Why did he
Why
Why
Why
Who's there?

V.

She is confused. The sun climbs high. My hair bleeds through the tangle of her face. No nose, no eyes — just blood burned obsidian-hard and a great open mouth torn with teeth, tongue scrabbling like a worm. I stroke my hand along her ruined jaw. She twitches. With pain, alarm or want I cannot say.

Some call me a cruel thing. Because there are laws carved out by sun and sand. Because I am of them, and because I must abide them even when they are unfair.

Still, I am not without a little heart. Nor do I lack a voice. Her ears have crumpled out like ruined shells, but she may hear me. I am a Desert, after all. And she will know my ways as well as I can measure out her heart, and all things that remain for her.

I'm here.
Speak, child.
Tell me what has been done to you
And I will understand.

VI.

I'm going to die. Out here
Where it's so hot and dry.

It wasn't supposed to be this way
Not this time, not again.
Not when he said I was so pretty
in the dress that he picked out.
It was his mother's, he said.

He said so many things
I can't remember and
I don't know anymore if I
should have cried or laughed.
Or what I'd do now if I could.

He said he'd never touch like that
like light beneath the door
like Venetian blinds dicing up a little
silver slipper moon that looks
so much like a rag doll's face.
Hands in my lap, hair down my back
I listened.

He said he'd never speak like that
words that cut knife-lines against
my wrists and ankles. He said he
would be kinder than my family,
the girls who choked down laughter as
I passed, text books against my tiny breasts.
Eyes beneath my glasses, eyes wide open
I listened.

He said he'd never hurt like that
head pressed against a wall, nails
raking down a neck while knees divided
what should have been indivisible.
Mouth shaking now,
I spoke
I spoke and I said 'yes' to everything;
his hands and eyes, his teeth and tongue
his feet, his fists, his scars
even, at last, this dress
until, eventually, I was a mouth.
A swollen mouth; red lips, hot tongue
a line of jagged teeth to bite
all I could get and chew it down.

I did not chose this place
I never did.
I just wanted everything and more
the things other girls got so easily;

a pair of arms,
a house with four walls and a roof
the moon in the window on my wedding night
and not to be afraid.

I wanted, God
I wanted so many things.
And now, and now
I'm going to die out here because of that.

I wanted
I wanted
I still want
Can't you see?
I want I want
I want, without a no
I am a mouth of yes, I want
without a no.

VII.

There's nothing I can do. The sun is hot and I hear the growl inside. Inside I scry her cells, weak from the baking blood, parched from this place. Too soon, the mitochondria will die. Too soon she'll sleep and all of us will feast. That is the law and purpose of this place, the law that's scribed in stone and in my sand. I cannot change it any more than I can change myself.

Still, sympathy is not forbidden me. Neither is love. The wind blows hard against her tattered dress, lifting it away. I over blow and wrap myself against her, warm and, I hope, comforting enough.

Don't fear me, child. I am a simple thing.

I am a thing of sand, and sun, and life unseen or spoken for.

I am the wind in the sage
I am the heat on the rocks

I am the silence before dawn.
I am the desert, I know how to hold
And I know how to want.
I will give you what you seek.

VIII.

IX.

And all the rest is lost. She falls into a trance. Her mind is tossed with these; a wedding dress, two green and smiling eyes, a bush, a brush, a bed, the slicing moon, and finally her face caught in mirror. I draw a breath. She was so beautiful.

Hush, sleep.
Don't fear the heat.
Don't fear the sand.
Don't fear me.
Let me sleep here with you.

There follows sun.
There follows rain and wind.
There follows hunger
And an end to hunger.

I cannot measure time as it streams through us.
Time is only, after all, the passage of the light and heat.
And what is that to us?

I sleep inside her arms, inside her throat
inside the ribs that covered her hopping heart
like a wedding veil.

We sleep here and I slowly bleach her bones
whiter than silk
whiter than wings.

Erzebet YellowBoy
Moonstone

THE QUEEN OF HOUSE WILLOW had only one fear; she clutched it tightly to her and it mastered all of her days.

It had begun with the burning of the willows. They had been there since House Willow's founding; in a time lost to history the trees became the namesake of the people who grew to glory with them. They had wept their branches into the young queen's hair as she played beneath them as a child. Nestled safely behind their curtain, their grove also became her only haven when childhood was left behind. And now they were gone.

Her chair creaked as she rocked softly in front of the mirror. In its reflection she noted the moonstone that rested in the curve of her throat. It had been carved with delicate strokes in the shape of a willow's leaf and was as old as the House itself. Some said it had been bespelled, that it bound its wearer to the trees. The queen did not know what had caused the binding. All she knew was that those trees had been a part of her, and she a part of them.

She noted, too, the mound of her stomach as it pushed against the soft fabric of her gown. She smiled as her hands smoothed over the happy curve.

"My lady," said an attendant. "Your tea."

"Most kind," replied the queen, as she lifted the warm cup with two hands.

From within her belly she felt a small foot push against her flesh. She touched the tiny isle appearing in a sea of silk and the fear rippled along her spine.

* * *

NOT SO LONG AGO there had been a king who ruled beside her. A queen should have a king, her people demanded, and though she cared little for the idea, she agreed for the sake of her House and those who depended upon it. She let her advisors choose, trusting them in this as she did in all things. She believed that they would not err. She learned too late that they had.

He had come from a distant shore and, while pleasant enough at first, soon proved to be a harsh and greedy man. He cared only for taxation, for fine wines, for gold. He wanted his queen beside him, his trophy and his security. He did not understand her devotion to the willows and chafed at the hours she spent in the grove. Though the queen bore him for as long as she could, on that horrible day when she watched as the grove was engulfed by flame and burnt to ash by his spite, she cast him away. She bade the court magician to curse him, a flame for a flame he shall have, and she banned him from her realm. As the king scuttled through the gates, he returned curse for curse.

"As you have taken your House from me, so I will take from you what is mine," he spat. The queen put her hand to her belly and stared him down, but when he had gone she fled to her rooms and cried.

The queen turned from the mirror and the memory and raised the teacup to her lips.

IN TIME SHE GAVE BIRTH to a set of lovely twins, a boy and a girl. The babes soon grew into dark hair, bright eyes and rosy lips that gaped in a toothless smile whenever the queen entered the nursery. The twins spent every moment together, hardly knowing where one ended and the other began. She had an enormous playpen built for the pair of them. It was well padded on the bottom to protect them from falls, with mirrors caught on the inner sides to enchant the twins with their own gazes. On the outer sides of the playpen the queen had instructed the court magician, he being skilled in all manner of astrological workings and matters of the spirits, to inscribe runes and sigils meant to insure the safety of the twins as they played.

They were given two of each toy, though this did not prevent the inevitable rivalry between them. If one twin picked up a silver rattle, that would surely be the rattle the other coveted and its mate would lie ignored in the corner. The queen smiled at her children as they clutched their chubby hands around the noisy toy and struggled over its possession. Eventually one would pry it from the other, leaving the other to howl in fury. The twin who had won the rattle would then immediately pass it to the empty-handed twin, for that was the nature of their bond. One would give anything to ease the other and the queen would give anything to keep them safe.

When she could not attend them herself, the queen made certain that their nursery was filled with ladies and lords, maids and men, all there to watch over the children as they played. The queen gave her children all of the love she had ever felt for the willows and more, and hoped to see a new grove grow up with them.

One day, like any other day, the queen was called away from the nursery for some official duty that she would rather have left untended. Being the queen, however, she would not put her realm aside, so she arose from her great chair as the twins continued their combat without concern.

So engrossed were they in play that they did not notice when, one by one, their attendants nodded off to sleep. As they stood or as they sat, their heads dropped to their shoulders and they froze as if under some terrible spell. When the last one succumbed, a small, untended door that had been locked for as long as any could remember creaked open, the iron padlock wafting to the floor in a flutter of dust.

The twins paid no heed as a small figure crept through

the door and stole its way to the side of their pen. The runes lit as though from a fire in the wood and the sigils began to hum. With a wave of an arm the inscriptions sizzled and burnt away and only then did the twins turn to see a hooded man looking in upon them. They gazed at him curiously, for what did they know of fear? Not until the gnarled figure reached in and snatched the girl away from her brother's side did they both begin to cry and shriek. Quickly the stranger tucked the girl under his arm and ran from the room. They vanished through the small, wooden door as though they had never been, leaving the boy alone and screaming in the big playpen, now so much bigger without his other half beside him.

The thief took the girl through hidden passages and tunnels until he was far out from below the castle and then traveled on until he reached a secret place he had prepared far in the back of a cave. He placed the queen's daughter in a small and ugly playpen where he left her all alone.

Oh, how she cried! Tears ran down her face to gather at the bottom of the lonely pen, creating a puddle there. She cried so hard that the water from her eyes dripped out of the crude pen and onto the floor. She wailed and screamed at the top of her lungs, but no one came. She cried until her tears made a small stream leading out of the playpen, across the floor and out of the room in which she was being kept. She cried until there could not be a drop of moisture left in her eyes, yet still her tears fell.

In the nursery her brother echoed her cries. The queen had returned to find the attendants rubbing their eyes in confusion, one of her precious twins missing and the other screaming in a frightened rage. Though she held him and tried to calm him, nothing would ease the child. His tears also began to create a small stream, one which flowed down the queen's skirts and between the floor stones and away from the nursery in which the twins had played all of their young lives away. He cried until there could not be a drop of moisture left in his eyes, yet still his tears fell.

The queen, stricken with grief, could do nothing for either twin. One was gone and the other could not be soothed. Powerless, paralyzed by her loss, she could do no more than sit and rock her remaining twin in the hopes that she would somehow be able to ease his anger and fear. She rocked him back and forth until a groove began to wear into the floor. Her attendants came and went while the queen held the boy and his tears flowed into the stream that went unnoticed by all.

What the queen feared had come to pass and she, upon finding one of her precious children missing, had sent out huntsmen and hounds with the scent of the girl in their noses. It was her only hope and what she believed to be a futile one, for anyone who could bypass the magic carved into the sides of the playpen was surely no one who could be tracked by hounds. Indeed, every evening the huntsmen sent back a report that no trace of the missing twin had been found.

The two streams grew as the tears of the crying twins fed them. The boy's tears wound their way out of the castle, across the field and into the forest nearby. The girl's tears wound down out of that secret place in which she was kept, across a field and into a forest nearby.

The waters crept ever closer to each other through the briars and grasses and trees, until finally the two streams met and joined in a hollow in the wood. Such was the nature of their bond, that even their tears, given freedom from their bodies, could not remain apart. There in that hollow a small pool began to form.

On a warm evening the queen's huntsman returned to the castle to make his report. He told the queen again that no trace of her daughter had been found. The queen bowed her head, thanked and dismissed the huntsman, sighing as she rocked the crying boy. She noticed, after a moment, that the huntsman had not left her side. She gazed at him in question and he cleared his throat with a nervous cough.

"I apologize for remaining in your presence," he offered, "but I am troubled."

He described what appeared to be a rather sudden change in the surrounding landscape of the castle. He reported that a stream was flowing from between the rocks of the castle and that, upon finding this stream, he had followed it. He apologized again, for in his following he had disobeyed her orders to track her daughter, but his curiosity had been aroused. The queen bade him follow the stream to its end and to report back to her his findings.

The following day the huntsman returned to her with his news. He had found that the stream led to a pool, more pure and fresh than any he had ever seen. This pool was being fed by not only the stream that led from the castle, but by another coming from the opposite direction. Strangely, the pool had not been there before. He had been frightened and returned. The queen thought about this for a moment. Her eyes strayed to the boy, still crying in her arms. She noticed for the first time that his tears were flowing out across the grooves in the floor, snaking under the doorway that been long forgotten by all. Suddenly she sprang up.

"Call the horses!" she shouted. The queen handed the crying boy to a nearby maid and ran from the room, the huntsman at her heels. "Watch him well!" she called behind her as they sped to the stables.

Swift horses were made ready and they mounted with haste, goading the animals on. The huntsman led and the queen followed, clinging hard to her poor beast's mane. To the stream they raced and beside it they continued, through the fields and the forests to the pool he had found. There they stopped and as the queen watched the two trickles of water that fed the pool, she was overcome with fear. She turned her horse and followed that other stream, riding the creature to exhaustion.

As she suspected, the far stream led her and the huntsman right to the hidden cave where her daughter had been taken. As she pulled in her reins at the entrance and dismounted, she saw a thing that froze her heart. The stream that had been flowing from inside the cave had stopped and the water was slowly seeping into the ground. The queen gathered her skirts and raced into the depths of the caves before the water vanished entirely and there, in the very back, she discovered the small, dirty pen.

All was silent as she reached in and lifted out the warm body of her daughter. She curled the small form into her arms and placed a kiss upon her forehead, but the child did not stir. Then, the queen saw that though the body was warm, the spirit had fled. The girl had stopped crying only when she could cry no more and her tiny soul had slipped from its confines.

The queen's eyes glazed and she opened her mouth in a scream that roared across the lands as the huntsman stood by helplessly, watching her voice her pain. Finally, still clutching the body of her daughter, the queen climbed wearily onto the back of her horse and turned towards home. Upon reaching the castle they were met by a group of her ladies, each one with a look of horror upon her face. They led the queen with her bundle into the nursery, where the twins' playpen sat empty, all the while not saying a word.

The nursery, as the cave had been, was eerily silent. The queen simply looked at the pen and then turned to the crib the twins had shared. There, on the soft bedding, lay a body as small and as cold as that of the one in her arms. One of the ladies, perhaps braver, or more compassionate than the others, explained to the queen what had happened in her absence.

"Some time after you left," she said, "the boy stopped his crying."

The maid who had been rocking him came and told the queen that the instant the tears stopped, she had looked to find that the boy had gone, his tiny soul slipping from its confines. Nothing they knew could revive him and so they dressed him and placed him in his bed to await her return.

The queen gazed down upon the face of her son and then at the face of her daughter, so alike they were that even in death they could not be told apart. She carefully tucked the girl beside the boy and, as she stepped back from the bed, the girl's hand slipped into her brother's.

"You will build them a bier," she said to the magician, "near the pool their tears have made. There they will rest until I return." And then the queen looked him squarely in his eye. "I will restore House Willow," she promised and strode from the room.

The magician, a stout and friendly little man under ordinary circumstances, went immediately to the small pool in the forest where he cast a mighty spell. So badly did he feel that his magic had failed to keep the twins safe that he tried to make up for all of his errors, both real and imagined, in the making of their bier. From a flute he blew glass in the shape of a small boat, within whose filigree every animal there ever was chased clouds woven in amber lights. Fishes from the sea and dragons from the air danced among the strands and he caused the ship to float above the still waters of the pool as if sailing for the sun.

He adorned it with the stars and caused purple colored mosses to grow within where the twins would rest. When the last of his spells wisped away into the wood, the twins were brought from the castle, hand in hand, and placed gently on the moss. With one last act, the magician pulled from the air a blanket made of no material ever seen by man. The fabric waved delicately on the breeze, its golden folds shimmering lightly as the magician, with a tear in his eye, laid it over the bodies of the twins.

The queen, meanwhile, had ridden a fresh horse back to the cave in which her daughter had been found. There, she entered into its dark crevices.

"I know you are here!" she cried, as she passed the pen in which her daughter had shed her final tears.

At the back of the cave was a tunnel that she followed until ahead she saw gray shadows on the cold rock. She let the light guide her to a small chamber where she found what she had come for.

He huddled over a fire. Its wavering arms illuminated the rags and debris strewn about the floor and the worn robes wrapped about him. He raised his head to the queen.

"I knew you would come," he said.

"What choice have you left me?" she asked.

"Oh, you have had many choices, but you have rarely made the right one," he sighed as he stepped up to her, so that his breath rose in the air and brushed her cheek.

She wanted to recoil, but did not. "I want them restored to me," she said, believing that some foul magic had taken them away.

"And what of what I wanted, oh mighty queen? Only to rule by your side, and to have my own small part in your House."

The queen shuddered, remembering. "And you could have had it, had you not disturbed my wood. It was your act and none other that set you where you are now."

"No!" he roared. "You chose those silent trees over me! It was your magician that cast me out in this shape, who left me with no recourse but to hide away from all men! You ordered this!" With that, he let his robe fall from his head and the queen saw, for the first time, what had become of her king. Scars covered his body, as though he had been horribly burnt. Almost, she felt pity.

"What must I do?" she asked.

The king's teeth bared in a grin. "Finally, you are the

one to beg for a scrap from my table. Let me think a moment." He turned away. The queen closed her eyes. She knew his price would be steep.

"Your precious twins," he sneered, "cried mightily for each other. I notice they did not cry for you. At the bottom of their pool of tears lies a single black stone. You, and none other, must retrieve this stone and bring it to me."

"I will," said the queen, and she left him there.

As the queen approached the bier that the magician had created she knew a moment of awe, but she also knew that she had to go about her business quickly and so shook his spell from her.

She tore the gown from her body and dove into the clear waters. The pool was deep, but the queen did not care if her need for air overcame her. She could not give up. Just as she felt her lungs could take no more, she reached the grassy mud at the bottom. There lay a black stone just within her reach. She grabbed it with shaking fingers and thrust herself to the surface as her breath exploded from her body.

On the bank she rested, wondering at the plain thing he had asked for his price. The queen suspected foolery, but had no other hope. She wrapped her gown onto her body and jumped astride the horse, the stone clutched firmly in her grasp.

There, in the cave, she presented the stone to the king. "Well done!" he said with glee. "Very well done. I did not think you could swim, my dear."

The queen gritted her teeth, but spoke calmly. "My children."

"Let's not be hasty," he said. "I am not sure this one little stone is worth the lives of your brats. I think there must be another stone, a red stone, resting at the bottom of the pool. I think I require it, as well."

Here was the foolery, but the queen was prepared to do all in her power to have her children restored to her.

"Very well," she said.

She returned to the pool where once again she removed her garments, worn as they were from her riding, and lay them on the bank. She did not bother to look at the lovely bier, knowing already what she would see there. She jumped immediately into the water and went straight for the bottom.

This time the search did not go so well. The waters were cloudy, her breath did not hold and it took several trips to the bottom before she held in her hand the king's price. The red stone dried on the bank as the queen allowed herself a moment's rest, but only a moment passed before she mounted the horse once again and returned to the cave.

She threw the stone onto the floor at the king's feet. "There is your stone. I want my children."

Slowly he reached down and lifted the object, inspecting the cracks filled with dirt. "It is, indeed, the red stone that I requested," he said. "You are to be commended for your persistence."

He shook his head. "I am afraid, however, that it is not enough. Are not the lives of your children worth more than this?"

"Take my castle, my lands, anything you want of me!" the queen cried. "Ask and it is yours, if you but restore my children to me."

The king laughed. "Now," he said, "now that it is far too late, you want to give me your realm. I think not, my love. You may keep it."

The queen bowed her head.

"No, not the realm. There is but one more thing I require of you. You should find it an easy task after all you have done so far."

"What is it?" she asked, exhaustion flooding her bones.

The king giggled madly. "At the bottom of the pool there lies a pure, white stone. Return here with that in your hand and your children shall be restored."

71

The queen did not believe him, but this was all the hope she had. She turned towards the pool one last time.

Down again she dove, her heart weary and her limbs almost numb from the cold. Seven times she had to rise for air and seven times she swam back down, determined to find the stone. Finally she saw it, glinting in the weeds, a pure white stone the size of an egg. She reached into the murk to pull it out, but just as her hand closed around it the earth below her trembled and the stone split in half.

The queen watched, dazed, as from the broken shards there rose a woman whose limbs shone white as the moon and whose hair spun away from her head in waves of silver.

"Why do you trawl for rocks on the bottom of the pool?" she asked in a voice full of the watery deep.

"The rocks are the price of my children's restoration," said the queen, mindless of the air quickly leaving her lungs. "I want no more than to be with them."

Bubbles filtered from the strange woman's lips as she smiled. "No magician's trickery can restore your children to you. You have seen where such as that leads. Why are you still following?"

"What else can I do?" the queen asked.

"Water drips away and rocks are broken. Only roots hold firm. How will you hold your children now?" asked the strange woman. "The white stone will restore your to you children, but you are looking in the wrong place," she said as she melted into the reeds, a last, long frond of her hair drifting across the queen's neck.

The queen raised her hand to brush away the woman's hair and instead touched the moonstone, still in its golden setting, shining white in the murky deep. She felt the shape of willow in the stone and the answer became clear. She let the last rush of air escape from her lungs as she dug her feet into the muddy earth at the bottom of the pool. With what strength she had left, the queen drew upon the magic that had been carved into the moonstone long ago. She closed her eyes, thought of how good it was going to feel to hold her children again and reached up for them.

The waters of the pool rolled and roiled and grasses floated to the surface, only to be sucked back down by the whirls which formed, spreading from the center outwards to lap at the bank. Slowly, like a vast creature surfacing from the depths, from the center of the pool rose a willow tree whose branches encircled and covered the bier until nothing of it could be seen through the leaves. The queen held her twins and would not be parted from them again.

The king waited, but the queen never returned with the white stone as he had demanded. His ire grew, for he was certain that he could dangle her on the end of his promises indefinitely and he had looked forward to doing it. When it became obvious that she was not returning after all, he wrapped himself in his robe and went to the pool himself.

There he saw the willow, great and green above the dwindling waters, hardly more now than a few puddles resting within the roots of the tree. In the center of its bole, as if grown there with the bark, was a single moonstone, shaped in the form of a leaf. The king grew so angry that he cursed and pulled at his hair, tore his robe from his misshapen body with a shriek and stamped on it, twirling about. His rage reawakened the Queen's curse; the tenor of his screams changed as a fierce flame erupted to consume his pitiful flesh. His ashes fell at the foot of the willow and soaked into the ground.

When next the ladies and lords of the court came to pay their respects to the royal heirs, they were all shocked by the sight of the willow and marveled at the rebirth of the grove. All but the magician, who was not surprised, who knew true magic when he saw it.

Helena Bell
Bluebeard's Second Wife

He wishes I were like his first wife:
Queen, domestic goddess with the small hands
and curling eyelashes. Neck like a willow branch.
His beard turned blue, lamenting
that I cannot talk, nor cook, nor breathe
like she. I'll purge her slowly.

The drapes must go. Silver she touched.
Her kin in town will move. Any tastes
we share, I'll change. She liked dogs?
I'll stuff the menagerie with cheetahs,
pluck feathers off her squawking parrot
and shove it naked in my cats' teeth.

He'll resist at first. All men do.
Shift her belongings to the fourth hall closet,
bar the entrance. Doubt my will.
But I will not rest,
until there are no rooms left.

Jo Walton

Post-Colonial Literature of the Elves

We have been your hedge-row boys,
Your hobs, your leprechauns, your children's toys.
We bring you magic dresses for the ball
When once our ancestors were seven feet tall
Smiling and bowing under your oppression,
We suffered shame and terrible depression.
We capered at your whims, brought magic junk,
And all we were and all we could be . . . shrunk.
Our history, our dignity, our worth
Almost forgotten. Once we ruled this Earth
With beauty, pride and honour in our ways.
We grant your wishes, live our petty days,
Smile, smile, and bring you potions where you sup
And plot rebellion in a flower's cup.

Richard Parks
A Pinch of Salt

N O MATTER WHAT STORIES you've been told or what you'd like to believe, the fact is that a mermaid can never forsake the sea, at least not for very long. Forget the gills and the tail — there are ways around those obstacles. Usually those ways are of the magical sort, with conditions and taboos and other rot, but even that is beside the point.

JUST THINK OF HUMAN BEINGS, whose blood is only distant kin to the ocean waves, measured in a pinch of salt. Consider how we yearn for the sea, travel on the sea, live by the sea, swim and splash in the sea, even feed off the sea like pups at the teat. Consider this, and think of a mermaid's bone and blood, solidified foam and the endless night of the abyss. Consider all of this, and you'll understand why the mermaid Aserea, after seventeen years of a very loving marriage to Jal the Fisherman, simply walked down to the beach one bright summer day, regrew her gills and fine, iridescent tail, and disappeared forever.

You must understand that Jal didn't do anything wrong. He didn't beat Aserea, or spy on her as she bathed, or any of the other conditions that had been placed on his happiness. He was kind and caring and Aserea loved him deeply. The problem was that Aserea was a mermaid, the sea called her back, and when she could no longer resist the summons, she obeyed. Leaving Jal to grieve and their sixteen year-old son, Makan, to rage.

"Why didn't you tell me that Mother was a mermaid before now?"

"What business was it of yours before now?" his father asked calmly enough, mending his nets to try and take his mind off his loss. That didn't help, of course. He'd been mending his nets on the very day he had first spied Aserea, washed up on shore and helpless after a storm. He'd saved her life and in her gratitude . . . well, that is old business and need not concern us here.

"What business? She was my mother!"

Jala worked his marlinespike deftly. "And you would have been born of a woman whether she was once a mermaid or not. Besides, your mother and I agreed that the fewer people in the village who knew of her origins, the better. She was here, and that was enough. Now that she isn't, you're entitled to know why."

For several moments Makan could do nothing but stare at his father who, all the while, continued to mend nets with a sort of brooding intensity that might have made Makan hesitate to say what he said next, if he'd been of clearer mind.

"Don't you feel anything? Don't you *care?*"

The marlinspike hesitated on a bit of cord, then resumed its work. "'Care,' the fool says . . . You try to spend every moment with the woman you love, year after year, knowing to the core of your soul that each and every moment might very well be the last and all your tomorrows come to be drowned in those depths. Try that, Son. Try it for one sodding day."

"Father — "

The bung had been pulled and Jala wasn't stopping now. "Pray, you who understand so much — what would you have done, knowing that your mother paid for every moment of your happiness with pain and longing? Would you ask her to stay? Would you tell her to go? Find the balance for me between one cruelty and the other, because your poor father never could. But you didn't have to, did you? Oh, no. You swam in the ocean and climbed the trees and hills and learned to notice and chase after the village girls, and never once — once! — suspected that perhaps, just perhaps, the world did not revolve around you."

"There must be something . . . " Makan began, but Jal stopped him.

"Nothing. Your mother is gone. Think of her as one dead if it helps. She'll probably do the same for us." He finished his repairs and tossed the heavy net to his son, almost knocking the young man into the sand. "I suspect that it's time for the yellowheads to be running off Snakepit Island. Take that net out and see if you can catch any."

"What are you going to do?" Makan asked, regarding the net with distaste.

"I'm going into town and I am going to get drunk. Feel free to do the same when you're older. It won't help, but you're my son and you'll probably do it anyway. If you mention your mother to me again in that tone you'd better be prepared to fight me."

"I won't, don't worry," Makan said, sullen.

His father sighed. "Don't promise what you can't fulfill," he said, looking wistfully out to sea. "That's why I didn't ask you to promise. Neither am I going to ask you to swear to what I'm going to ask now."

"What is it?"

"Aside from your thick skull you're basically a decent young man, and that being the case, sooner or later you're going to fall in love. It can't be helped. I only ask that you try not to fall in love with a mermaid. For both your sakes."

JAL HAD BEEN RIGHT ABOUT THE YELLOWHEAD. They were schooling in large numbers and the surface of the water was nearly boiling with them. Makan was just about to cast his nets when he was startled by the sound of a woman singing. At least, he thought it was a woman. The voice sounded at once female and like nothing he had ever heard. The sound was enticing — it wanted something from him.

Makan wasn't sure what that might be, but he wasn't really thinking about it.

"If the song is coming from Snakepit Island, then some poor woman has been stranded there and needs help. I had best look into it."

Makan reluctantly put his father's newly-mended net aside and steered his small craft closer. Snakepit Island wasn't a lot more than the tip of some submerged mountain. Its shores were steep and craggy and there were very few places to make landfall. Not that there was much reason to do so--there was little vegetation and what meager fresh water there was came in runoff down the central peak and varied considerably from year to year. The island was fit only as a rookery for seabirds and the colony of adders that had given the island its name. They had established themselves there somehow or other in the distant past, feeding mainly on the smaller birds and the occasional egg.

While the island itself was of little use, the waters around it were a favorite spawning ground and news of the yellowheads' presence would not be a secret for long. Makan knew he needed to make his catch and head home before the fishing grounds became too crowded to work easily. Still, he had to check on the singer first.

As he got closer to shore he finally saw her, perched up on the edge of one of the lower island cliffs, perhaps no more than ten feet above the crashing waves. The poor thing had apparently lost her clothes in the wreck and she was, so far as Makan could see, completely naked.

He lost sight of her for a while then which, he thought, was probably for the best. The approach to shore was difficult, even for one who knew the way, and Makan concentrated on keeping his skiff off the rocks as he steered it through a crevice in the side of the island and into a very small, sheltered bay. Makan tied up his boat carefully and climbed up through a crack in the rock that was the only exit out of the landing.

The woman was perched on the low cliff where he'd seen her last, her legs tucked beneath her as she sang. Her back was to him and Makan realized he had never seen so much bare female flesh in his life, including that of his mother and even the more adventurous village girls. For a moment all he could do was stare. Such was his preoccupation with the curve of her hip and the play of the light across her back that it was several seconds before he realized that she didn't have legs tucked beneath her. She had a tail.

"Mermaid!" he shouted.

The creature jumped almost a foot into the air and landed a bit awkwardly. She tried to scrabble back toward the edge of the cliff but in a moment Makan had taken two long steps forward and grabbed her wrists.

"Let me go, you oaf!" She tried to bite his hands but Makan pulled her wrists apart and held her at bay, her arms outstretched. It was difficult, though; she was much stronger than she looked.

Now that she was facing him Jakan noticed what he hadn't before--besides the obvious--that she was young. Probably, at least by appearances, no older than he was. And that she was very beautiful. Her hair was black and very long, and her eyes were a shade of green he was certain he had never seen before. It was hard not to stare at her, but he made the effort.

"I don't mean you any harm. I'll let you go after I've asked you a question. I just want to know if you've seen my mother."

The question seemed to startled the mermaid nearly as much as his sudden appearance did. She stopped struggling and looked at him more closely. "Your . . . mother?"

Makan nodded. "She's a mermaid, too."

"Oh. I guess that explains it."

"Explains what?"

She sighed. "Why you're not *dead*, of course. When I saw you coming I expected you to steer your craft onto the rocks off shore trying to reach me, and drown."

Now Makan frowned. "I admit you're very pretty, but why would I do something so foolish?"

She shrugged then. "Human men do it all the time. We're flattered, of course, but the drowning part seems rather self-defeating."

"It's your song. Mermaid songs drive fishermen and sailors to their doom. Everyone knows that. Since my mother was a mermaid, maybe it doesn't work on me." He hastened to add, when he saw just a little fire in her eyes, "I mean it was a very beautiful song. I just didn't feel inclined to kill myself over it."

She shrugged her small shoulders. "I'm not especially inclined to harm anyone. But I'm not going to stop singing."

"Even if people die?"

"Now and then our folk get tangled in your nets. Are you going to stop fishing?" she said.

"Fishing is how we live!"

"And singing is how *we* live. It's a peculiarity of our kind that we can't sing under water like the whales do, though our singing does carry under the waves; it's how we bedazzle the fish so that we can catch them. They're faster than we are. Or did you think we ate human flesh?"

"There were rumors," Makan said frankly. "But Mother never seemed inclined." He had to admit that the mermaid had a point about the singing, if what she said was true, and he rather believed it was.

"Please let me go. I've been out of the water a long time and I've used almost all of my breath singing."

"You still haven't answered my question--have you seen my mother? Do you know of her? Her name is Aserea."

81

The mermaid frowned. "It's a very large ocean and my people are very scattered. I'm sorry."

Makan sighed and released the mermaid's wrists. "Forgive me. I just miss her, that's all. I wanted to know that she's all right."

The mermaid looked suspicious. "You're actually letting me go?"

"I said I would."

She actually blushed slightly. "I know, but . . . "

Makan just shrugged. "I'm sorry if I frightened you and I certainly don't blame you for doubting me. If our roles had been reversed I'd probably still be trying to bite you."

The mermaid smiled then. "If our roles had been reversed that would have been wise, but then when you looked into my eyes you would not see in me what I see in you. Farewell."

Makan thought of asking her to explain what she'd just said, but didn't wish to delay her longer. "May I ask your name before you go?"

"May I ask yours?" she returned.

"Makan. Mind my nets, as I'll be using them here later."

"Gaena. Warning taken."

"Pleased to meet you," Makan said, but Gaena had already dived into the sea, the splash of her leaving lost in the crash of waves against the island.

THAT EVENING GOBLEC THE TAVERN KEEPER sent for Makan to come fetch his father, and Makan walked straight into the village and came back stooped over, the burden of his drunken father heavy on his back. He propped Jal against the wall of his room long enough to get the older man's boots off, then put him to bed.

Jal opened an eye. "What're you doin' at the tavern?"

"We're not at the tavern. We're home now. Go to sleep."

"I don't 'member walking home."

"You didn't. I carried you."

A faint smile from his father. "There's a good son."

"No more," Makan said. "You're done now. All right?"

Jal just yawned. "How was the fishing off Snakepit?"

"Good. I got a late start, but still managed to fill the boat. I was the first, so it fetched a good price."

"Why were you late?"

Makan thought about not telling his father, but didn't see much point. "There was a mermaid at Snakepit Island . . ." Jal was struggling to sit up, but Makan pressed him down gently. "It wasn't Mother. And I didn't fall in love with her, don't worry."

Jal looked relieved. "At least she didn't sing. Could have lost you, boy."

"She *was* singing. It didn't bother me. I mean, it was pleasant enough, but it didn't bother me."

"Then you're the first."

Makan shrugged. "I've got mer-blood in me, remember? We figure that's why."

"We? You *talked* to her?!" This time Jal did sit up, despite Makan's best efforts.

"Of course. I wanted to know about Mother. Gaena didn't know anything, though."

"Gaena. Heavens above . . ." Jal's manic energy seemed to desert him and his head fell back on the pillow. "You're either the bravest man I know or the stupidest."

Man. It was the first time his father had called him that. Not "young man," just "man." Makan wasn't entirely sure his father had meant that as a compliment.

"If you want to grieve for Mother still," Makan said. "Find a way other than Master Goblec's wares. We can't afford it and I'm not going to carry you home every night. You're heavy."

"Whatever you say, Son," Jal said, and drifted off to sleep.

83

THE NEXT DAY JAL DRYDOCKED the new boat he and Makan had spent so much time building together and began repairs on his former work boat, which he re-christened "Aserea." Considering the condition of the old hulk, Makan thought it rather an insult to his mother's memory even as he offered his help. This offer was cheerfully refused.

"You've got your own fishing to do. Since you're to inherit the *Windhorse* I don't want to add any more wear and tear to it; this old boat will be quite good enough for me in my declining years."

Makan sighed. "If you're in decline, then I'm a halibut. And I like the boat I'm using now. Stop this nonsense and take out the *Windhorse*."

Which was true enough. Makan had built his work boat himself, and while not as stable in rough seas as a larger craft, it was more than large enough for one person and all the fish he could manage. Jal insisted, however, and nothing else was said on the subject of mermaids or boats or, to be accurate, much of anything for the next several days as Jal made the old boat seaworthy.

The yellowhead were still schooling off the shores of Snakepit Island and both Makan and the once again sober Jal cast their nets alongside most of the rest of the fisher-folk of the village as long as the catch was good. Then, as suddenly as they had appeared, the fish vanished and the impromptu fishing fleet dispersed to wherever gossip or instinct took them. Some went east to the Turtle Isles. Others turned south to work the coast.

Makan lingered for a little while off Snakepit as he pondered what to do. He had just decided to sail north when he noticed a sinuous figure ride high up the cliffside on the ocean swell and then pull itself out of the water and climb up onto the ledge as nimbly as a snake. It was only when the figure turned and beckoned to him that he realized it was Gaena. He waved back and made his way to the island where the mermaid waited for him on the cliff.

"There are elders of our folk who have met nearly everyone, at one time or another. One knew your mother."

"You asked for me? That was very kind of you."

Gaena blushed slightly. "Well, it was no great difficulty. And it seemed important to you. I didn't learn very much, I'm afraid. Only that she had disappeared from our ken for some years; those who knew her suspected she'd died. Then she returned recently, only to vanish again."

"Vanish?" Makan felt a faint welling of hope. "You mean she might be returning?"

Gaena shook her head. "I mean she left this part of the ocean. She told her friend that she was going but not where. I gather that she said she never planned to return. I'm sorry."

Makan sighed and released the last of his stubborn hope like a butterfly that didn't wish to be free. "It's all right. I'm done being angry at her. She was wise to leave as long as there was the chance, even very slight, that she would meet my father again."

"Would that have been so terrible?"

"I don't know what it would have done to her," Makan said. "As for Father, I think it would have destroyed him."

Gaena seemed to consider this. "Sit down," she said, finally. "My neck's getting sore looking up at you."

"Oh, sorry." Makan found a flat place on the cliff's edge beside her and sat down. Gaena gave him an odd look.

"You actually did it. That's very trusting. It's not wise to be so trusting. You hardly know me."

Makan looked down at the sea, and the rocks, and conceded that, if Gaena wished him harm, this was the perfect spot to arrange it. "No, but I knew my mother."

"I'm not your mother," Gaena said primly.

"No, and I never saw my Mother in her true mermaid form, but I have to think she would have looked a lot like you. It's not just the tail, and not just the face, though she was beautiful, too."

Gaena rested her chin on her arms. "You shouldn't throw those words around so casually," she said. "Words have power. I hear that this word, spoken often enough, will make a human woman fall in love with you."

"I don't think I've ever made someone fall in love with me," Makan said. "And certainly not on purpose. Odd thing, though, but I think it is the women who don't really believe that they are beautiful are the ones who like to hear it the most. I wonder why, if they consider it a lie?"

"Very few women really believe that they're beautiful, deep down. Even the ones who know better," Gaena said. "So it's a nice sort of lie. No matter. Your flattery does not move me."

"It wasn't flattery," Makan said, frowning. "It was the truth."

She shrugged. "You believe in your own lie. All the more effective."

Makan scowled at Gaena for several long moments before it finally sank in that she was teasing him. He blushed.

"That was unkind," he said.

"Perhaps a little," she agreed. "I'm still mad at you about the song."

"Because I didn't die?"

"I said I didn't want to harm anyone and I meant it, and our songs are for the purpose I stated and no other. That doesn't mean that we're not a little pleased when human men risk death to reach us; I said as much before. Who wouldn't be?" She must have noticed the shocked look Makan gave her and she continued, defiant. "You seem to appreciate the truth, so I'm telling it. While the mirror and

86

the comb legend is overblown, that doesn't mean we're without vanity."

Makan thought of many things to say, and thought better of each one until he was finally left with the one thing he did say: "We can meet here every three days and I can tell you how beautiful you are and how well you sing. Would that make up for it?"

"I don't know," Gaena said, looking thoughtful. "Perhaps we should try it for a while and see."

SEVERAL WEEKS LATER, instead of setting out at his usual early time, Makan's father was waiting for him at the docks. "You're going out today," Jal said.

Makan shrugged. "Aren't you? The weather is good."

"I mean you're going to Snakepit Island. Oh, yes. I know about that. Lokan passes there on his way west and he's seen you three times or more."

Makan shrugged again. "So? What business is that of his?"

"Or of yours?" Jal asked pointedly. "The fishing is poor there now and will be at least until fall. Or have you developed a sudden fondness for snakes?"

"I'm going to meet Gaena," Makan said. "I assume that's what you weren't asking me." He hadn't realized he was going to say it before he did, but he didn't regret the words once spoken.

"You're a fool," Jal said.

"Perhaps," Makan agreed.

"Perhaps? You know how this will end!"

Makan shook his head. "That's the thing, Father — I don't know how this will end. I don't know what this *is*, yet. I'm sorry, Father. I know you mean well and have my interests at heart, but whatever happens between myself and Gaena is something we're going to have to sort out for ourselves."

Makan braced himself for a fight, but there wasn't one. His father had simply sighed, called him a fool again, and mentioned that it wasn't Makan's fault, really, since the condition seemed to run in the family. He did ask that Makan pick up a length of rope that the chandler had set aside for him. Then Jal untied the *Aserea* from her moorings and sailed out of the small bay. After he'd run his father's errand, Makan followed.

It was a beautiful, clear day, with nothing but blue sky and a few wispy clouds visible. Makan steered toward Snakepit on a favorable wind. As he approached the island he saw another craft on the same course.

It was the *Aserea*.

"What is he . . . "

Gaena was singing. Her voice carried clearly over the water and, frankly, Makan didn't think she'd ever sounded better.

"Bloody hell!"

Makan's boat practically skipped across the water, but the *Aserea* was too far ahead. He'd never reach it in time. He shouted at his father to change course, but of course he didn't. He shouted at Gaena to stop singing, not certain if she would hear him or heed if she did. Jal was not half-mer; he was simply human, and Gaena's song would be irresistible.

Father's going to die. And there isn't a damn thing I can do about it.

The realization left him numb for a moment but quickly led to panic. He thought of trying to steer in front of his father's boat, but the *Aserea* was too far ahead. Perhaps he could get close enough to catch his father's boat from behind with a grapple . . . and then what? Have the *Aserea* pull him onto the rocks too?

If I drop my anchor as soon as the grapple hits . . .

Makan didn't really think it would work, but he had to

try. He got the grapple ready. He was closing on the *Aserea*. Just a little more . . .

In the rush he almost didn't notice that Gaena had stopped singing. Now Makan could see his father clearly in the stern, his hand firm on the tiller. "Father! Turn starboard!" he shouted, almost giddy with relief. Without Gaena's song, there was still time —

The *Aserea* did not change course, and Makan never did get close enough to use the grapple. He threw it anyway, but missed the stern of his father's boat by several yards. In another few moments the *Aserea* broke its back on the rocks. Makan would have followed, but his grapple snagged on something and his own boat shuddered to a halt so quickly that Makan was thrown overboard just a few feet from the rocks. When he broke the surface again he saw the *Aserea* slipping beneath the waves and no sign of his father. The only other thing he saw was Gaena's lithe form, diving from the cliff into the sea before the waves pushed him against a rock and the world went dark.

MAKAN REGAINED CONSCIOUSNESS to find Gaena leaning over him. "Not drowned?" she asked.

"No. Al — almost," he said. He spat out seawater and coughed. Gaena pounded his back until the fit passed.

"Oh, no. Father . . . !"

"He's right here," the mermaid said. "I don't think he's drowned, either. I pulled you both up but he hit his head too and he's not awake yet."

They lay side by side on top of the low cliff. All Makan could think at first was that Gaena was indeed much stronger than she looked. He turned to his father and confirmed that, yes, Jal was breathing. Makan slapped the older man's wrist until he opened his eyes.

"Makan?"

"I'm here, Father."

The older man coughed a few times and tried to sit up. "You saw . . . Your mermaid almost killed me!"

"I did see. She's not 'my' mermaid and she saved both our lives, you liar. You owe her an apology. We both owe her thanks."

"Liar? How dare you speak to your father that way!"

"How? Easily, when I consider what you just tried to do!"

Jal looked away. "I meant to try one more time to talk some sense into you, and then I got pulled in when she started singing, that's all."

Makan turned to Gaena. "Is that true?"

"I suppose," the mermaid said. "Once he set sail for my island, he must have heard me then."

Makan nodded. "Meaning he was too far away to hear your song until he deliberately steered toward the island. Father, you had plenty of time to reach the island before I did. You were waiting on me!"

Jal turned beet red, but Makan already knew it was the truth. Jal growled, "And what if I did? I had to show you what she is!"

"I know what she is, Father. So do you."

Gaena looked from one human male to the other, the frown on her face deepening by the moment. "It's rude to talk about someone in front of them, you know," she said.

"I'm sorry, Gaena. I think Father meant to kill himself and use your song as an excuse to do it."

"I meant to go look for your Mother," Makan said. "Even though I knew it was useless. Then I found out about you and this . . . person, and thought of a better way of throwing my life away. I figured at least this way maybe my death would bring you to your senses."

Makan shook his head. "You're no martyr, Father. This is about your pain, not mine."

"I didn't want you to make the same mistake." There

were tears in the older man's eyes.

"Mistake? Father, look at me and tell the truth. If you had it to do all over again, when you found Mother helpless on the beach. Knowing now what you didn't know then? What would you do?"

"I — "

"What would you do?" Makan repeated, relentless.

Jal closed his eyes. "I'd have done the exact same thing. Heaven help me, but I am a fool."

"Why? Because you refuse to give up the happiest time of your life? If that's a fool I'll take a dozen. Why would you deny me a chance at what you had, even if, yes, it was only for a while?"

Jal looked like someone had punched him in the face. He finally put his face down in his hands. "I never meant . . . ."

"I know."

"Can you forgive me?"

"I'll think about it." Makan then turned to Gaena. "Gaena, do you love me?"

"Love you? I'm not even sure I like you at the moment. Between you and this crazy old man, I may never get any fish."

"I'll be sure to bring you some. Now answer my question."

She looked at him. "Suppose I say 'yes.' What then?"

"I don't know."

"Yes, you do. So does your father, and so do I. That's why I'm not going to say it. Neither are you. Promise?"

"I can't do that."

"I know," she said, and reached up and kissed him. It was a kiss that felt at once too brief and yet endless, and for a moment they both felt what the promise meant, and that word was loneliness. Gaena turned and dived headlong into the sea.

"I'll be here tomorrow," Makan said softly, but the sea made no answer.

Deborah P. Kolodji
Siren's Call

Come dance with me
in the autumn Sedona sun
where solar rays strike red rocks
with the aura of a vortex.
A portal opens
to our own private world —
sizzles of electricity
surround us as we cavort
in primordial frenzy.
My nipples respond
to the increased earth energy
as we salsa on the mesa
and tango in the heat
to the beat of a rattlesnake.

Come dance with me
on the ice of Europa
as Jupiter casts its shadow
where the sun is distant
and the surface is smooth.
Our skates trace our initials
for the next space probe to ponder
then you lift me up
and we glide forever
my weight in your arms
lighter than on Earth.
There is no air to breathe here
yet the magic of our choreography
is enough.

Come dance with me
beneath the ageless sea
as the currents of our lives

flow into each other
among the ghosts of shipwrecks
and bioluminescent eels.
We shimmy in gulf streams,
wear nothing but garlands
of sea anemones,
synchronize our strokes
in an underwater ballet
that pleases us even
as the white shark circles.

Come dance with me
in zero G as our spaceship
approaches Venus, veiled
beneath swirling clouds
of mystery.
We spin like sixty-nines
in an upside down universe,
caress whatever part
of each other we can reach,
giddy from our lack of gravity.
The tug of the planet
overpowers us as we fall
helpless to the power
of an aphrodisiac world.

Come dance with me
the song echoes at Stonehenge
among the standing stones
where there are no more druids
to hear my message of seduction.
I whirl naked in the moonlight
according to an ancient ritual
and embrace the darkness.
Somewhere, in some century,
there is a man, listening.

Ekaterina Sedia
Simargl and the Rowan Tree

W HEN HE DIED, he was handed a fiery sword and an absinthe spoon. He tucked the former under his leather belt, and gave the latter a careful looking over. No doubt, the spoon in question was his own, the very instrument of his demise. He run his fingers over the feathered slots of the antiqued silver, and thrust the spoon into the back pocket of his jeans, his elbow encountering an unexpected obstacle in the shape of a pair of wings. He then turned to the faceless luminous figure that endowed him with the accoutrements of the afterlife.

"What do I do now?"

"You guard heaven," the figure said, and gestured vaguely in the direction of the endless azure expanse, where a golden chariot idled, waiting. "Your name is Simargl. Follow Ra."

That explained the wings, then.

Simargl nodded his agreement, and headed down a steep aurora borealis to the waiting chariot that cradled a giant, glowing orb. A man in a hawk mask, the driver of the chariot, gave him a slow nod. "You must be our new Simargl. Welcome."

"What happened to the old one?"

"Nobody lasts forever. Even I am getting old." The sun god heaved a sigh. "So, I presume you have killed yourself by fire?"

"It was an accident," Simargl replied, the spoon in his back pocket flaring hot at the memory. "But I suppose it was self-inflicted."

Ra clucked his tongue, and the chariot started to move, slowly at first but soon gaining speed, forcing the new

Simargl to trot after it. "This is what Simargls are," Ra said. "Suicides by fire."

The day went on, as the chariot arced through the blue plains. As he trotted along, Simargl noticed that running was much easier on all fours, and that a fiery aura had grown around him. As far as he could guess, he looked more like a winged dog than a man. Just as Simargl started to fear that the azure void would never end, a green glittering jewel caught his eye. When they got closer, the green turned into a fresh meadow, studded with white and yellow flowers, sliced through by a sparkling stream. A cow — a gleaming white cow, and the most beautiful creature Simargl had ever laid eyes on — grazed among the flowers sagely.

"This is the Celestial Cow Zemun," Ra said, and pointed at the wide berth of tiny white stars that stretched above the meadow. "That's the Milky Way — she made it."

"Hello," Simargl said.

The cow smiled, with a mischievous twinkle in her emerald eyes. "Ah, good. It is about time you got here. Just make sure you do your duty, and don't give into the lure of the middle world."

"I apologize for my ignorance — " Simargl started.

"I forget that you've just got here," Zemun interrupted. "You're in the upper world — not because of virtue, but as a result of the manner in which you died, understand. The middle world, Yavi, contains the living and the lesser beings — banniks, domovois, rusalki . . . they are not enemies, but don't be distracted by their charms. And then there's Navi, the land of the dead and Chernobog, and his general Viy." The cow gave a thunderous sigh, and her eyes moistened. "My daughter Dana is married to Viy's son, who stole her from me."

"I'm sorry," Simargl said.

"Don't be," said Zemun. "Just watch over us, so that Navi's evil doesn't seep through to heaven."

And so Simargl did. He followed Ra's chariot all day long, and at night they usually arrived somewhere else — Zemun's meadow, Belobog's tall castle, or Veles' forest. But wherever he went, he found his gaze straying downward, to the middle world. His vision became such that when he focused on an object, no matter how remote, it stood before his eyes, diminutive but in perfect clarity. He could watch children playing in the gardens, the rusalki swimming and frolicking in the cool waters of the autumn streams, and the bird Sirin's solemn flight, as it sought to harvest souls and carry them to Navi. At night, he never slept but watched the wonders that unfolded in the lower worlds.

It was only the matter of time before his attention was returned. One of the rusalki, a gaunt girl with transparent eyes, the soul of a drowned virgin, looked up at him and smiled.

"Simargl," her voice whispered, disembodied and hollow, ringing out in the empty heaven, "come to our feast, come to our rusalii... we will play and sing all day, and we will wind long garlands of the water lilies. Come and dance with us, fire dog with the golden fur."

"I can't," Simargl said. "I am guarding heaven."

The girl sighed. "Oh, surely you can sneak away just for one night?"

"I wish I could," Simargl said. "Besides, I don't know how to get down."

"That's easy," the rusalka said. "Just find the rowan tree and climb down the trunk."

"Maybe some other time."

The rusalka's transparent eyes stared upwards, straight at him, but he wasn't sure if she could really see him. "Tell me about heaven," she pleaded.

He did. He felt bad for her, for how much she longed to be up there, but was instead bound between the world of the living, and the cold riverbed that was her grave.

She whispered about the rustling sound the small stones made when the current of the river rubbed them against each other, of the long strands of algae that entangled in her hair, of the small curious perches that came to peck at her dead eyes, and cried. "Why can't I see heaven?" she said between sobs.

"I died too," he told her. "I was a man once. But I died by fire, and ended up here . . . "

"It's a painful death," she said. "Perhaps this is why you went to heaven and not me. Perhaps I did not suffer enough." Her eyes glistened. "Tell me how you died."

He explained to her about the absinthe ritual, of how one poured bitter liquor over the sugar lump cradled in the spoon, and lit it on fire. He told her of the sizzling sputter of caramelized sugar, of the slow drip of liquor and melted sweetness through the slots of the spoon. He should've been more careful, he admitted. His balance was already affected by his previous intake, and his motions grew languorous and clumsy. He knocked over the silver goblet and the spoon that rested atop it, spilling the flaming, sticky sugar and absinthe mix over his clothes. It burned through his clothes and his couch, caught on the curtains, and the sizzling he heard all around him smelled of charred flesh.

He spoke to the rusalka, whose name was Kupalnitsa, every night. But he never ventured downward. His presence in heaven seemed too important, even though he did keep his eye out for the trunk of the rowan tree stretching between the worlds. He found it one day, when Ra stopped for the night. It seemed that with every day their trips were getting shorter, and Ra hunched more in his chariot. He rarely spoke.

Their resting place that day was a forest, deep and cool, buzzing with mosquitoes. Ra sighed and dismounted from his seat in front of the chariot, leaving the sun in its cradle parked in the narrow opening between tree trunks. He lay on the cushion of moss under a tall spruce, and closed his eyes.

Simargl watched his companion sleep, surprised and saddened to notice how old he had grown. With a heavy heart, he turned away, and decided to take a stroll to take his mind off Ra's decline. Among the tree trunks, he meandered, never fearing to lose his way, since the sun shone brightly like a beacon in a dense forest. And then he saw another source of light — a column of pure white, streaked with red and yellow.

It was the rowan — the world tree, and its branches studded with ripe red berries stretched above his head, and its trunk pierced the forest floor and continued down, deep below through Yavi, all the way to Navi, the underworld. It was dark there, and the fur on his back prickled: even from this distance, he saw the misshapen creatures that shifted in the darkness, he heard the weeping of the dissolute dead, he smelled the stench of the foul river that carried the dead souls to their destination. And then he saw Viy.

Viy's eyes were concealed by the eyelids so long they brushed the black sand under his clawed feet, and his fingernails scraped and tore the ground with every step, as they dragged along. Simargl's upper lip curled and he gave a low growl of warning. Viy heard him, and motioned for his attendants, who carried iron pitchforks, to come closer and lift the terrible weight of his eyelids so he could look.

Simargl jumped away from the tree, uncertain what would happen to him if Viy's stone eyes met his; he regretted his interest in the underworld, and decided to confine his attention to heaven and Yavi only. Still, the weight in his stomach told him that he had made a mistake by drawing the attention of evil he thought to repel from heaven.

RA WAS GETTING WORSE. He was barely able to climb to his seat in the mornings, every joint of his desiccated body creaking with the effort.

"That's enough," the Celestial Cow decided when one night they spent their rest time in her meadow. "You son can take up your work."

"But I can do it!" Ra protested.

"No you can't," Zemun said, and looked to Simargl for support.

He had no choice but to growl in agreement. "Every day, we're traveling less. The day in Yavi is getting shorter and shorter. It's only December, and their nights are longer than days."

Ra slumped. "If that is to be my last day as the sun's guardian," he said, "I want to die. I don't want to be a useless old man. Zemun, old friend, lift me up on your horns."

The Celestial Cow lowered her mighty head obediently, and with a single toss the old god soared high on her horns. He bled from the wounds where Zemun's horns had broken his skin, and his blood flowed freer and wider, changing from almost black to clear. As the blood — water — flowed, Ra shrunk, and soon there was nothing left but a calm wide river, spilling from Zemun's meadow all the way down into Yavi.

"Ra-river," Zemun said. "It is better this way."

The two of them stood, watching the immobile sun reflect in the calm surface, and then they drank from the river. With every sip, Simargl felt the secret knowledge stirring within him, growing like a tree from its tiny seed until the order of the world stood clear before his mind's eye. Then, he summoned Khorus, Ra's son.

Khorus was young and strong, and he didn't want Simargl's help. So Simargl found himself free to wander as he pleased, and he took advantage of it. His fiery sword in his paw, he walked across heaven on two feet, making sure that evil did not seep through. He spent most of his time in the forest near the world tree. There, he could talk with

Kupalnitsa as if she were right there, next to him, and he could see her clear eyes as if they were level with his face.

She cried and pleaded, and begged him to come down to Yavi, to dance at her pretend wedding; she would never have a real one. She whispered of the dark desires that blossomed in her chest — terrible urges to steal the babes from their cradles, and to lead the passersby astray. Crying, she confessed that she was with the other rusalki when they found a child, lost in a wheat field, and tickled him to death.

"I can't come to your wedding," he said.

"Navi would be better than this!" she cried.

"But maybe I can help you." He reached up to the branches of the rowan tree with his clawed paw, but still the berries hung too far. He picked up his fiery sword and swung, and the berries fell into his open palm like drops of blood. From his drink of Ra-river, he learned that the berries had many mysterious powers. "Take these. They can cleanse the smudges of sin from human souls."

He opened his paw and watched the berries roll down the trunk, and fall one by one into Kupalnitsa's cupped hands. All but one — a single berry avoided her, and kept rolling, all the way into the darkness of Navi, where it disappeared like a stone in a deep well.

"Thank you," Kupalnitsa whispered, and swallowed the berries. Their effect was instantaneous — her eyes gained color, the palest blue of the autumn sky, and her gaunt face lost its hungry look.

Simargl sighed with relief — he could not take her to heaven, but he could help her battle whatever darkness was taking her over. Berries seemed like a small price to pay for saving her from the terrible fate of the rusalki, and he tried to ignore the nagging worry about the single berry that rolled into the underworld.

He patrolled heaven as usual, nodding to Khorus who

occasionally crossed his way on his repetitive trip, and to Zemun, whom he visited often. The Celestial Cow was the one who brought it to his attention that things were not the way they were supposed to be.

"Something stirring in the underworld," she said one night, as they were playing one of their frequent games of marbles.

"How do you know?" Simargl asked.

"Just a feeling I have," Zemun said. "The same one I got when Viy abducted Dana for his son." She pushed the bright yellow marble with her muzzle, and it collided with Simargl's favorite, a clear one with a blue spiral inside. "I didn't pay attention then, but now I do. The only thing worse than an old fool is an old fool who doesn't learn. I know Viy is up to something."

"It's probably nothing..." Simargl's regretful gaze followed his favorite marble as Zemun swallowed it. "But I accidentally dropped one of the berries from the world tree into the underworld."

The Celestial Cow gave him a troubled look. "Is that so? Oh Simargl, you may have caused a misfortune! Why did you touch the world tree?"

Stumbling over his words, he told her about Kupalnitsa and her plight, of her fear and hatred of her nature.

The Cow nodded. "I understand. Your gesture was noble, but it had an unintended consequence. You must rectify it."

"What can I do?" Simargl sat up, huffing, the game forgotten. "Besides, maybe nothing will happen. And if Viy had got that berry and ate it, I have no way of retrieving it. The best I can do is to keep my eyes open and guard heaven."

"Perhaps," the Celestial Cow said. "But know this: the berries have strong magic. If you wait too long, the problem might be greater than what you can handle."

"I'll go tomorrow," Simargl said with a sigh.

"Good. Ra-river will lead you. And drink of its water on your journey — Ra will make you wise. Rest now."

When Simargl awoke the next morning, he noticed that something was amiss. He rose to his hind legs and stretched, as Zemun slept peacefully in her meadow. It was cold; colder than he could ever remember. Moreover, it was dark, and Simargl worried that the evil had struck.

His suspicions were correct. When he resumed his vigil, not a few steps away from Zemun's meadow, he found Khorus, his mask splattered with dark blood and his throat slit. The empty chariot rested next to him.

Simargl cried over the dead god's body, his heart rent by guilt — there was no doubt in his mind that Viy was able to enter heaven with the help of the berry, legitimately, and this was why Simargl did not sense his presence. When his sobs had died down, he returned to the meadow, and told Zemun of what had happened.

Without words, the Celestial Cow broke off one of her horns, and it became a large barque, with richly decorated hull of mahogany and amber, and the sails spun out of silk. The masts of the barque, the tallest of cedars, seemed to pierce the low, leaden sky.

"Follow the Ra-river," the Celestial Cow instructed, "until it leaves Yavi and flows into the river of the dead. Keep a look out for Viy's fleet."

"I'll bring the sun back," Simargl promised, and set on his journey. His only provisions were the jug of Ra-river water and a handful of rowan berries.

The barque floated down the river, slowly as it traversed heaven, and speeding up as it approached the precipitous drop off its edge. The barque stood at the top of the waterfall for one tremulous moment, and then plunged downward, falling among the froth and sparkling waves all the way to Yavi.

Simargl caught his breath when the barque righted itself and resumed its dignified progress down the Ra-river. Its waters darkened, and he felt uneasy under the leaden sunless skies, boiling with angry clouds.

The inhabitants of Yavi shared his discontent — he saw them all along the river, people and demonic creatures, their gazes turned to the sky, their faces lined with unease. Men and women, children and old people keened and complained. The bowlegged satyrs and the green-haired mavki, domovois and leshys, banniks and kikimoras all gnashed their teeth and cursed those who were responsible for the missing sun.

Their anger and grief touched Simargl, but there was only one face he searched for. Kupalnitsa was not among her sisters. Once or twice he thought he glimpsed her pale face underwater, and wondered if his visions resulted from guilt and longing. Still, he called out her name a few times, but no answer came. He looked at the water, trying to glimpse her again, but the river had turned muddy and foul, and slow menacing shapes moved below the surface — skeletal fishes and undead whales trailing threads of slime and rotting flesh.

When Simargl looked up, he realized that he was underground; the light was the same as in Yavi orphaned by the sun, grey and cold. The stone ceiling cupped low over the barque's masts, and dangling beards of lichen and mold soiled the white sails a putrid green. He remembered Zemun's warning when he noticed long sleek shapes darting in and out of the rolling fog upstream — the Viy's fleet, a flotilla of long sleek boats fashioned from dead men's nails.

"Simargl," ominous voices whispered all around him. "Turn back, turn back, fiery dog. Navi will swallow you, drink your blood, splinter your bones . . . there's no fire here to protect you."

The hairs on his back stood on end, and a low growl pulled back his lips. Still, Simargl stood on the prow, the fiery sword clenched tightly in his paws. His gaze tried to pierce the darkness of Navi, to find the hidden sun and its abductors, but the stone walls and hissing in his ears rendered him almost blind. He could only clutch his sword and keep his eyes on the Viy's ships.

They approached, slowly, cautiously. Simargl discerned the dead who manned the oars, and small demons that tittered and rolled around, and leapt high. On the prow of the main ship sat the bird Sirin, its feathers sparkling green and blue. The bird had the face and breasts of a woman, and it sang.

Sirin's song was the most beautiful thing he had ever heard — it rolled and trilled like a brook born of snowmelt running over stones, it promised and reassured that happiness was close. He needed only to close his eyes and give into the sweet voice. His knees weakened under him, and his hands lost their grip on the hilt of the sword. He fell into her words like a stone into a well, welcoming oblivion and sleep. Sleep was happiness, and he only had to close his eyes, to lie down, and he would be home, away from the sunless sky and dead eyes of the demons. As he sunk to all fours, his front paw touched the blade of the sword, and he hissed in pain — the blade burned deep into his skin, jolting him to awareness.

Simargl took a quick gulp of the water from the jug, and felt the calm wisdom of Ra radiate through his mind, clearing his head of the curse. He chewed on the berries, their tart and bitter taste fortifying his weakened body, and sprung to his feet. The flaming sword in his paw flared brightly, sending the demons scuttling for cover and whimpering in fear.

Sirin stopped her singing and hissed in frustration, and the ship that carried her swung around and disappeared into the fog. Simargl followed the fleeing ship, until he came to the beach covered in black sand and empty shells of hermit crabs. Simargl leapt out of the barque, and chased after the shapes that laughed and skittered in the dusk of the underworld.

"Simargl," came a tiny whisper from behind him, "wait."

Kupalnitsa, her face stained by the foul water but unmistakable, smiled at him as she swam to the shore.

"Where did you come from?"

"I latched onto the keel of your boat as you passed through Yavi," she said.

Her words about Navi being better than her fate were fresh in his memory. "Will you stay here?"

She shrugged, and twisted the hem of her long linen shirt to squeeze out water. "I want to see it first."

She followed Simargl as he left the black beach and entered the forest of phosphorescent, leafless, weeping trees. Their crooked branches entwined over their heads, forming a cupped canopy.

Simargl kept peering through the dense entanglement of trees and black brambles. He noticed a weak beam of light penetrating through the growth, and turned toward it. But the light did not come from the stolen sun; in a forest clearing, covered with yellow grass, a fine red cow chewed her cud.

"Dana?" Simargl said.

The cow nodded.

"I'm friends with your mother," Simargl said.

Dana's brow furrowed. "Mother?"

"The Celestial Cow Zemun. Don't you remember?"

Dana shook her head.

"Give her a berry," Kupalnitsa said.

Simargl offered the cow a berry that glowed bright red, like a ruby. Dana swallowed it, and her eyes went wide.

"Do you remember now?" Simargl said.

Dana smiled. "And I miss her. Can you take me with you to visit her?"

"If I get the sun back," Simargl said.

"I can help you!" Dana pointed with her hoof. "Over there, it is hidden in Chernobog's castle. Viy guards it. But please, do not hurt his son, Pan — he is my husband. And remember, you can't hurt Viy with iron."

Chernobog's castle loomed atop a cliff that jutted from the forest like a giant thumb. The building itself seemed like an ugly growth on the rock. At the foot of the cliff, Viy was waiting, his attendants at his side, ready to lift his terrible eyelids. At the sight of him, Kupalnitsa gave a little cry and covered her eyes with her pale hands.

Gripping the hilt of his sword, Simargl approached the monstrous general.

Even though Viy could not see him, he spoke in the gravelly voice. "You came for the sun, guardian of heaven. And you've bested Sirin."

"Yavi and heaven needs the sun," Simargl said. "And the murder of Khorus and Dana's abduction will not be unpunished. Prepare to fight, Viy."

Viy's laughter, quiet but unsettling, scratched Simargl's very soul. "I'll fight," he said, and snapped his fingers, grating his nails. "Attendants, lift my eyelids!"

Kupalnitsa gasped. "Not his eyes! Simargl, he turns anyone into stone with his gaze!"

Simargl lunged at the attendants, his sword at the ready. He tried to chase them away, but as he swung the sword, he severed one of Viy's eyelids. No longer held down by its weight, it started to rise. Simargl shielded his eyes with one paw, and thrust at Viy with the fiery sword.

"To the left," Kupalnitsa yelled from behind him. With

only one eye open, Viy could only pay attention to Simargl. "Careful, he's got an axe!"

Something metal, of great weight whistled close to Simargl's floppy ear, and something warm trickled down his fur. He felt suddenly dizzy, and took a stumbling step back.

Kupalnitsa cried out directions, and he followed them blindly, thrusting his sword this way and that, and ducking whenever she told him to. He swung, and felt the burning blade encounter something solid. Foul blood spilled from Viy's wound, and he uttered a slow, halting hiss that froze Simargl's heart. The dark liquid pumped over the blade of Simargl's sword, and it hissed and sputtered, and then its fire went out — it was just a regular iron sword now.

You can't hurt him with iron, Dana said, and Simargl cast away the useless weapon. As Viy advanced on him, injured but still strong, Simargl retreated blindly. He was going to die again, and stay in Navi forever — not as Simargl, but as one of the countless grey souls that inhabited the underworld. The memory of his first death overwhelmed him, and he felt as peaceful as when Sirin was singing to him of quiet surrender, of wordless happiness. He heard the crackling of fire all around him, and felt a burning in his pocket.

The silver absinthe spoon was still there, and he grabbed it just as Viy's bulk pressed against him. He thrust the spoon at the quavering belly of the general, and Viy gave the most terrible of cries anyone had ever heard, and stepped back. Where the silver touched his warty black skin, a fresh wound bloomed, spreading open, growing wider with every minute. Viy's flesh sputtered and recoiled from the contact with silver. Simargl chased after him, all the way up the steep steps of the castle. At the doors, Viy turned around, and Simargl flinched and covered his eyes. He pushed the spoon at Viy's throat, drawing a deep moan from his chest.

"You won," Viy told him, his lone eyelid brushing the ground. "You can have your sun back."

Simargl walked through the Chernobog's castle, and found the sun in the throne room. The dark god himself scowled at him from his throne chair, made of skulls and thighbones.

Simargl bowed to the god, but his gaze was on the sun, sitting bright and unharmed in the middle of the bone floor, spilling its light through the narrow windows.

"Don't burn yourself," Chernobog mocked.

Simargl picked up the sun, but it didn't burn him, and instead clung to him like a child ready to go home.

Simargl carried the sun outside and placed it into the barque. Meanwhile, Kupalnitsa ran to fetch Dana, and the two of them sat in the barque with him.

"I missed heaven so much," Dana said. "I'm going to visit my mother often, now."

Kupalnitsa sighed. "I wish I could see it too."

Dana's blue eyes turned to Simargl. "What say you, guardian of heaven? Didn't this girl earn the right to leave Yavi?"

"I hope so," Simargl said. "I'll ask Zemun if Kupalnitsa can stay in heaven."

The barque left the black shores of the underworld and glided upstream, serene like a swan, until the caved stone ceiling of Navi and undead whales fell far behind. The inhabitants of Yavi greeted the return of the sun, and paid no mind to the fiery dog, a red cow, and a pale drowned girl who sat beside it in the marvelous barque built by the Celestial Cow.

Sonya Taaffe
The Marriage of Iphis and Ianthe

for Mary Renault, Sappho, and the best cousins ever

To meet her parents, they took a night train
through rain and London and the news of war,
hand in hand, sometimes. Cigarette after cigarette,
she smokes her way through Platonic ideals,
a dark-haired boy in pale lipstick
and a fisherman's sweater, brown-wristed,
tanned, as a bull-leaper in an ancient frieze.
Her hair brushed apple-russet to her shoulders,
she leafs through stiff sketches from life
and surgical anatomy, rain-beaded forsythia
laid aside from her blue-skirted lap
for skinless muscles or the crippled tendons
of a hand. Light flickers in at the panes
like film projected across their faces
as the carriage rocks through the silvery dark,
heroines of their own transformation
in mythic black-and-white, exiles
with no sure homecoming, no altar fires,
with no gods and goddesses unless the lover
who holds her other self close through the night,
as though each morning were the miracle:
to wake together what they always were.

The wedding night, the rafters raised high
as their cousins chanted bawdily outside the windows —
pine torches and spring flowers, Hymenaios and Hera,
hyacinth worried to a heartsblood stain

under her nails. Bridegroom, she kneels
in red wool, the stiff scratch of myrtle in her hair,
to her bride on geometric linens whose mouth
tastes of quinces and shy desire, encouraged
and afraid to touch her rose-shadowed, tawny
curls. All the shadows in the room are theirs,
no silent-eyed, sand-whisper deities
in the lamplit flicker on painted walls
nor the woman whose words rustled with grain;
no slip and slough of flesh refashioned
in this heat that wells between her thighs,
her breasts, her heart that claws at itself
for cowardice even as her fingers close
on pale-red petals that a thumbnail slices brown,
unfolding the face of her bride to smile
like any wondering boy at this beloved girl
who by moonset may not love her still,
lying alone as the Pleiades sink into the sea.

The subway rattles them home in the sunset
over the Charles River, tired with shopping
for groceries and used books — bean cakes
and bay leaves, Pushkin's name sponged
in gilt on the spine. She braids her hair back
blue as Poseidon, in sleeve-torn black T-shirts
stacks her canvases too high for the cats,
the swan, the laurel, the vine-choked ship
as stylized in spray paints and mutable
as once in red-figure and fired black.
Her glasses rimmed with fluorescence,
she catalogues eyestones, clay envelopes,
carnelian seals and goat-fish in porphyry
and she cut her hair like a chrysanthemum

after her doctorate, slashed peony-pink.
Their shoulders lean together like slices
from the same fruit, horns of the same moon.
When their hands clasp, the same silver rings
click against one another that linked
like a magic trick in their hearts: two
become inseparable one. And the toilet
needs plunging, one of their mothers
is a no-call zone on a yellow Post-It note,
the pregnant Siamese chewed up the jade plant
and half a postcard of the Phaistos Disc —

unnuminous, all. These commonplaces
their honeymoon brought like an oracle
from the justice of the peace, the sea
that drowned wax and wings: two women
in bronze-beaten sunlight laughing
like the moment when lovers become
all their hearts' metamorphic desires,
all the unaltered shapes of love.

Danny Adams
The Wind-Catching Wizard

O GREN NEARLY TURNED HIMSELF TO STONE to keep from recoiling in horror when the old wizard offered him a pouch of gold.

The wizard chuckled at his bodyguard's reluctance. "What's the matter, Sergeant Venn? You've earned it. Your men have earned it. This is your reward for good service."

The warrior shifted as if straightening a sword stance. "Ogren, sire," he corrected, though he had been in Gettir's service for four years. Venn was Gettir's bodyguard generations before Ogren was born.

"Yes, so I said. My apologies if I was mumbling again."

"And sire," the warrior said even more quietly than usual, "you have already paid us for this month."

Gettir blinked under his single white brow. He straightened the simple violet sleeping robe that he had taken to wearing throughout the course of every day. "Don't be foolish, Ogren. I'm not losing my mind. I . . . I'm . . . ." He stared at the bag in his hand as if it were about to come alive and bite him. "You misunderstand me. This is a — bonus."

"If you'll pardon me, sire," Ogren said, "You are already extraordinarily generous. My men, quite frankly, are hoping you live forever."

"Well, if not for yourself then, for your men. Spread it among them with my gratitude."

Ogren recognized face-saving when he saw it and bowed deeply. He took the bag of coins, thumbnail-sized varri, knowing he would be unsurprised if it did in fact bite him. Gettir retreated into his study looking as if he'd just learned about the death of an old friend.

Perhaps he has, Ogren thought, staring at the now-closed study door. *Gettir is as close to his mind as I am my muscle. I can't imagine being a withered old man dying immobile in my bed. Not that even my Peleshtam should hope to live so long. But the wizards, even the oldest of the Imradi — who knows how long they truly live? The mind can't hold out forever anymore than the body can.*

It wasn't the first time Gettir was forgetful. But Ogren had considered it no more than that. Gettir still had an incredible recall for the stories he loved telling, some tales centuries old that would have been long-lost but not for the Sire Wizard. Gettir was always busy, distracted — partly the reason he'd hired the warriors to watch his back. His mind was just elsewhere.

The word *elsewhere* chilled Ogren's spine.

He exited the keep as if the walls were closing in on him. Suddenly there was an acrid stench in the air he could no longer take — not the smell of mortality, familiar for as long as he could remember, but the of age, a rare treasure in his world, a blessing Ogren often prayed to avoid.

On the walls Ogren thought he'd remembered paintings that changed as their landscapes did, along with ancient golden chests holding balls of light or statues that changed what stone composed them at will. But now there was nothing but gray, fractured walls in every corridor, emanating only enough light for Ogren to flee outside.

He spent the rest of the day and much of the night in the courtyard with sword in hand and ignoring the curious stares from his men, who knew better than to talk to him while his blade was swirling faster than even they could see.

OGREN HAD INITIALLY THOUGHT the summons from the Sire Wizard Gettir four years before was a joke — not that he doubted a wizard might summon him, since many had before. It came with the territory of being a Peleshtam. No, what surprised him was the offered salary.

113

Kings and nobles paid their soldiers with bronze stobols. Wizards — most wizards — paid in silver andri. Gettir offered pouches of gold, usually varri, the highest-grade gold in the world.

One bag for Ogren to start, with three more to divide among his men, laid out in front of the long table of Gettir's Great Hall. The Sire Wizard, eldest of the Imradi, themselves the oldest wizards in the world, crossed his arms and scowled fiercely, a look Ogren had often seen from wizards, except this one was sincere. Gettir had no fear of Ogren's immunity.

"Peleshtam," Gettir said thoughtfully. "An old, old word, meaning many different things to different peoples . . . what is your translation, Master Ogren?"

Ogren shrugged. "It changes at need. Last year we called ourselves the Dragon Spears. After the Gell War a few months ago, we feel more like Old Hawks, so that's the answer today for anyone who asks."

The Imradi scowled. "I know you are magic-immune," Gettir continued, "but is it true that the Peleshtam also make immune anyone you merely touch?"

"It is true, Sire Wizard Gettir, as long as we don't break contact."

"Sire will do. Very well. Keep me alive and you will receive such pouches every month." He spoke in an unfamiliar rolling accent that Ogren discovered later was centuries extinct.

"Do you have a particular enemy in mind?" Ogren asked then. That was hard to imagine; Gettir was notoriously the most benevolent and philanthropic wizard in the world.

Now, the warrior reminded himself. *But someone may be harboring a grudge against him for a slight a hundred years gone.*

The wizard smiled thinly. "I just wish to be around as

long as I am able — there are so many books left to read, stories left to tell! You and your men will defend me against any enemy who may try crossing my gate. Am I understood?"

Ogren bowed.

"You and the rest of your Peleshtam have a broad reputation for honesty, master warrior," Gettir continued, "but I would have the oath of you and each of your men. That is the price for my gold. *Any* enemy."

They all agreed, and Ogren could almost hear every other wizard in the world let out an unhappy rumble. *Let them rumble*, Ogren thought. *If they wanted magic-immune bodyguards they should have offered gold instead of silver. For all that, let them call us by our proper name, Peleshtam, instead of that stupid insult Unmortals — as if we weren't even human.*

For four years Gettir had been the best of masters. He always gave Ogren time to track down more Peleshtam, those born with the mysterious magic resistance, when reports of them surfaced — not difficult, since those born with this immunity were usually objects of fear, no longer human — *unmortal* — and cast out of their homes. All of Ogren's men had come to the Peleshtam that way, usually happy to find a home.

Just as importantly, he gave Ogren a free hand and looked the other way when the Peleshtam did something more uptight wizards would have slipped into angry convulsions over — though in truth they never spent their gold any differently than any other soldiers — mostly ale and women, though some of them had an odd interest in tragic plays. Just so long as they stayed fit and alert.

Which was remarkably easy, all things considered. The lands outside the castle walls were troubled as sheer overcrowding put neighbors and allies on the verge of war with each other. But few dared attack the Sire Wizard.

Easy, Ogren thought again. So as if directed by gods peeved by his complacency, the circumstances changed.

Then Gettir was suddenly at Ogren's side, whispering, "Any enemy, master warrior. Remember your oath."

Ogren ground his teeth. Even if that enemy, as witnessed on the main approach to the castle, included the king, half-a-dozen of the world's most powerful wizards, and a full five thousand-strong legion marching behind them wielding red standards bearing a silver sword and shield in the center of each.

Maybe the extra pouch of gold really *was* a bonus.

GETTIR SCANNED THE PROCESSION as calmly as if watching white wisps of summer clouds, one of his favorite pastimes. "Prepare the defenses, Master Ogren."

"Forgive me for putting it this way, sire," the warrior said, "but what have you done?"

Gettir jolted and looked away vaguely, and Ogren had a terrible gnawing in his brain that maybe Gettir had gone out of his mind and done some great offense — perhaps even forgetting about it later. Finally the old wizard's eyes cleared and he shook his head fiercely. "Nothing! Nary a thing!"

"Then they're not here for war, sire?" Though such processions had only been heard of in legend, Ogren knew. The king's army had not traveled all the way from the capital with the red flags for wine and venison.

But they might be open to a parlay. "I'll speak with the king myself, if his majesty will speak with me."

Gettir's face fell into that grieving expression again. "Do what you think is best, master warrior. I — trust *your* judgment." The wizard flicked his hand and disappeared in a puff of brown smoke.

As always, leaving Gettir's castle made Ogren feel utterly exposed, an infant among wolves. Ogren was hardly helpless; the castle's power was just that all-enveloping. Not as usual,

Ogren turned back to study it: the sharp spires of the front emerged first from the brown stone of Mount Zerubal, the highest peak in the world and said to the be the oldest — and the deepest, stretching down to the core of the planet. Legends said that no weathering could erode it, no magic could crack it, and in fact, if the mountain fell, the world would follow. Other portions took turns showing themselves to the sun; today Ogren could see the wing built during the Old Orander Dynasty, a time of rounded gargantuan stones, tiny windows, and a rippled ceiling that resembled wind-waves on beach sand. Incongruously, the bulk of Gettir's castle was inside the mountain. When Gettir asked about this once, Gettir simply said that he did not construct the castle inside the mountain those centuries gone, the mountain invited itself to grow around Gettir's castle.

King Dechirer was indeed willing to speak with Ogren. As were the wizards, though they looked at him askance and cautiously. No surprise, and something Ogren was long used to, since even their most powerful spells would roll off him like a spent man off a red-woman. He inwardly snorted. He could still be stabbed as much as the next man, if not as easily.

"Sire," one of the wizards said, "the Unmortal has arrived."

"Peleshtam," Ogren corrected without a hint of rancor.

The wizard, a gaunt ascetic Ogren recognized as Molochi of the Varr, snorted. "And what is your translation of Peleshtam this month, dare I ask?"

"The Ghost Eagles, Master Molochi. More eagle than ghost, if you were wondering."

"Sit, Master Ogren," the king himself offered in the royal tent. His clothes were neither regal nor battle-ready, but loose-fitting hunting garb, brown slacks and boots with a similar tunic beneath a dark green vest, all still well soiled from an interrupted forest excursion. His hair was unbound and just barely wisped at his shoulders. His mouth quirked down in frustration but not anger, not yet. "Would you care for wine and venison?"

"Nothing for me Majesty," he said, glancing around. As he suspected, the heads of the six most powerful wizarding houses were here, each themselves watching Ogren closely. Five were frowning; the one smile came from Finlay, their youngest at something less than one hundred years old, who rose through the ranks quickly in the single nation where wizards were democratically elected.

"Nothing except," Ogren continued, "if you would, an answer to your presence at my sire's gates."

Dechirer characteristically shrugged off Ogren's directness. Kings came and went, but wizards (usually) remained. This one was more aware than most that his reign existed on the wizards' good graces — particularly the Sire Wizard's.

It was also Dechirer's way, and a relief to Ogren, that he never dallied with small talk. "We fear that Sire Wizard Gettir is becoming senile. Can you confirm this observation, Master Ogren?"

"My liege, speaking anything to such a subject would be a betrayal of my master's confidences."

Dechirer knitted his brow and leaned back in the simple cushioned wooden chair he used as a travel-throne. "I will be blunt, master warrior. If Gettir is losing his faculties he poses a great danger to us all — including himself."

"If what you say is true, Majesty, then what do you propose to do about it? If there is a spell to reverse such an ailment, I would happily offer whatever assistance you require."

"There is no spell," the king said.

"Not even a binding spell?"

"Whose binding spell could restrain the oldest and most powerful Imradi in the world?"

"He must die," said Taillade the Elemental, the oldest wizard in the world second only to Gettir.

Ogren placed his hand on the hilt of his sword. The king raised a single brow.

"Please hear us out," Finlay cut in. Reluctantly, Ogren's hand moved back to his side.

"This is known by every wizard from the time they become an apprentice," Taillade said. "Great power also comes with great personal risk, and this risk includes death should you no longer be capable of controlling your power. Do you know the Yakika Desert, Master Ogren?"

Ogren nodded once. As a prisoner of war he had, unlike most of his comrades, survived a forced march through Yakika. A surreal experience, survived not just through willpower but occupying his mind with something other than the endless dunes: Absorbing every detail of the ruins of ancient homes and other buildings, wondering about each life once lived inside, who would build lives in such a forbidding place.

"Yakika was once a tropical land filled with green and water. Until the Grand Wizard Strappato, in his dodderage, broke a cup of tea on the floor and shouted a curse. What is now the Wasteland of Moravan had a population of over one-hundred thousand until the Wizardess of the Lakes, Chiquete, lost her senses after falling and breaking her hip."

"This is no trivial thing we must do," said Sophia, head of the House of the Wind, gathering her flowing silver robe about her. "Normally a wizard will take his own life in a specific ritual suicide. But Gettir made it clear at the last conclave that he would never take such an action. He has forced us to carry this terrible burden ourselves."

"And you must see," Ogren told him, "that my men and I have sworn an oath to protect the Sire Wizard against any enemy."

There were tears in Finlay's eyes. "We do this because

he is our friend, master warrior."

"He has become my friend as well, Wizard of the Stories."

"You have no concept of what he means to us!" Taillade shouted. "Do you even know what a Sire Wizard is, Ogren? He or she is the wizard who is trusted with teaching the generations of wizards who follow. There is not a wizard alive today who was not Gettir's student. And we are taken from our parents so young we never remember them. Gettir was more than our master, he was our father."

"Then find a cure," Ogren snapped.

"There is no cure!"

"You will find my men and I do not give up as easily as you. I needn't remind any of you that we are Pelestham."

Finally King Dechirer spoke again. "We are aware, Master Ogren. You can appreciate the risk, I imagine, of me bringing a full legion and the wizards here when we are on the verge of war — for that matter, when our own kingdom is overcrowded and on the cusp of civil war. They could be needed elsewhere at any time, and their absence at a crucial moment in the proper place could be devastating." He let out a long exhale. "I know you also appreciate that you are only twenty-one against five thousand of my men and the six wizards."

"The Sire Wizard would also stand with us."

"This is a sad enough day — we are already bound to lose one great treasure when Gettir dies. Do not let your deaths be the loss of another."

Ogren faced him squarely. "If we break our oaths to Gettir, Your Majesty, then how could you ever trust us again? Our honor would be ruined. Not a one of us would prefer to live under this shame."

Dechirer started at the master warrior for several heartbeats, then tugged at his beard. "Do what you must," he said, as if giving a royal command.

* * *

OGREN FOUND HIS MASTER SITTING at the far edge of the library behind a massive stack of books as big as the Great Hall's fireplace. His chin rested in hands atop bony arms that now looked barely able to support the weight of his own head. Ogren couldn't remember the last time he had seen Gettir's arms uncovered by robes; they looked as fragile as fallen twigs in the middle of an endless drought.

And his eyes were elsewhere.

"They told you, didn't they?" Gettir said. "That I'm going crazy."

"I have spoken with my men, sire. We are still bound to our oaths."

"They're right — Taillade and the others of my brethren. I should have killed myself as soon as I realized — But I cannot. I am a coward . . . "

"Suicide is the coward's means," Ogren cut him off more vehemently than he meant to. "If I were to lose my strength, sire, or my legs, or . . . The courage comes in the enduring."

Gettir looked to the ceiling, then ran to a window so tiny it seemed his head would get stuck inside. "You won't take me!" he shouted. "I'll die before I let you kill me!"

When Gettir wailed the entire mountain shook, that mountain said to go to the core of the world, that no amount of years of weathering could erode.

It is one thing to hear a tale — a legend, bordering on myth — on the consequences of letting a feeble-minded Imradi's power wreak havoc. It is another thing to see a place like Yakiki, the results of such magical chaos unleashed. But it was still another, Ogren realized too late, to see it happened right before you.

Or beneath you.

The mountain split with small cracks that became

fissures that became yawning ravines, no doubt smashing pieces of Gettir's own castle within. The rumbling also threatened to shatter Ogren's ears until it abruptly went away — taking all sound with it. Ogren found himself strangely light-headed and when he walked to the wizard's side the slightest step nearly sent him sailing into the ceiling.

The eldest of the Imradi himself was frozen with a glaze over his eyes, so Ogren chanced a look outside, holding the windowsill tightly so no stray breeze would carry him out and over. And there was nothing below him.

Nothing at all.

The castle was suspended over a black pit that robbed sound and light from everything around it, save here in Gettir's own castle itself, apparently. The mountain had fallen into the earth and darkness crept up from below, eating at the edges of the hole, gradually wearing it away. Fortunately the king's encampment had not been swallowed — yet. But the hole was growing until Gettir's castle floated above the pit and King Dechirer and the others were scrambling to pack up everything that could be saved.

"Sire," Ogren said quietly, touching the ancient man's arm. There was a crackling of light arcing between Ogren's fingers and Gettir's flesh, but as always, Ogren himself felt nothing.

"My dear Ogren . . . ." Gettir's tone of voice was oddly wistful, unfamiliar. "I never really wanted to be a wizard — I should have been a storyteller. Magic is useful, but stories...I tried once, you know. When I was twenty. I ran away from my master. But my master was — very persuasive. I never tried barding again, but nor did I ever forget."

"If you had left wizarding, sire, you would have died a long, long time ago."

"Ah, but telling a good story, Master Warrior, is like catching the very wind." The old man's face drooped. "You cannot be much more than forty years old, am I correct? I am one thousand two hundred years old, perhaps that plus ten. This is antiquarian even for my kind. Your life is so short and difficult, you have every reason to wish for life. I have no excuse."

"Life needs no excuse," Ogren told him.

"And if I tell you to kill me? What if I declare that I have become my own enemy, and I must die?"

"The answer isn't that simple, sire."

"If I order it, you are bound to your oath. Or if I go mad you may be forced to defend yourself."

Ogren had no reply. Gettir was right on both counts.

Ogren glanced out the window at the expanding hole; at least the encampment seemed to have moved a safe distance away. Finally the warrior asked, "What are your orders now, sire?"

"To . . . leave me to my books for the afternoon. So many stories, I'll never have time to read them all now, certainly not before the siege begins. In whatever form the siege ends up crafting for itself."

Ogren stood erect while Gettir mumbled about another great siege in the past, the castle of the Tall Wizard Androthine, and how much that siege was like this one right down to the moldings of stone vines wrapped around the drawbridge as Gettir had in this castle. Ogren stopped short and wheeled around.

"Sire, if I may ask — would you have any quarrel with me inviting the Wizard Finlay to dinner tonight?"

"Finlay . . . ? Oh, I should think not. He's always such a nice, polite boy."

He waved his hand in what Ogren thought was a dismissive gesture, but there was a thunderbolt outside, and when Ogren looked out again a long, taper-thin stone staircase descended from the castle, across the chasm, to meet the other side.

* * *

"IF WE HAVE TO KILL HIM," Finlay said, "it will mean a wizard war. There hasn't been such a thing in over six hundred years. Then there will be no way to avoid sparking a larger war, things such as they are. We may be facing a new dark age, master warrior."

The youngish wizard was walking side by side in Gettir's gardens, hands wringing behind his back, with Ogren, who held his arms akimbo. For a moment they were silent, during which time Finlay seemed more interested in the flowers than the crisis.

"I don't pretend to understand how magic works," Ogren said. *I don't pretend to know how my own immunity works either*, he didn't add. He was already ten years old in his earliest memory, waking up in a devastated village, already immune to magic. Nor had he ever found a clue about where he came from or how he'd spent his childhood.

He shook off the memories for the larger task. "But I've seen magic craft great wonders. Miracles, even my men have said, as cynical as they are. I do not understand why you cannot cure my sire's infirmity."

"Everything has a season, master warrior. Gettir has simply gone beyond his. It happens. No magic can change that." He stared at Ogren darkly. "Just as many things are cut down before their own season has come."

Ogren couldn't help but think of the ruined homes buried in the Yakika Desert again — the images hadn't quite left his mind yet — and the Moravan Wastes. No, it was certainly not unknown for even entire lands to be cut down before their natural seasons were ended.

Who was he to deny the wizards their ancient traditions? Or for that matter, risk hundreds or thousands of lives if Gettir loosed his powers in madness? Perhaps Gettir himself even knew he was slipping four years ago when he hired the Peleshtam. Ogren had never pushed for a reason; he had simply worked and trained as always, and enjoyed his gold at the end of each month.

"What does the suicide ritual entail?" Ogren asked.

Now Finlay stared at him as if sizing him up. "The *Lacere*. A voluntary final release of a wizard's power from the body, supervised by other wizards to make sure it is gradual and not destructive. I am told — I have heard from those who attended the last words of these wizards — that it is akin to a great stone being lifted from your shoulders that you never realized you carried until it was off."

"So the power builds within them over time rather than being channeled from another source?"

"Correct. At Gettir's age his power is great indeed."

"What becomes of this power?"

"Nothing. That is the point."

"And this kills the wizard."

"It isn't quite so simple. The loss of power in itself is not fatal; the magic slows aging but does not sustain the body in itself. But the wizards who have surrendered it thus surrendered all else. They had never known anything else. Without it they owned no more wish to live. Would you care to live deprived of your limbs and your sight and hearing and touch?"

Ogren shook his head slowly, but his mind was drifting back toward Gettir's library. "What would you say to me, Wizard of the Stories, if I gave you and the other Master Wizards permission to come into the castle and perform the ritual, and prevent the wars at the same time, on two certain conditions?"

"I should demand to know what the conditions are. Officially. Personally, you've piqued my curiosity."

Ogren explained his idea and Finlay was a long time in responding. At length Ogren asked, "Will the others agree to this?"

"If I can convince them it will work. And it will have to be me, though they still consider me a whelp. If you approach them they will believe that your loyalty to Gettir is setting them up for a trick — pulling out his power while he retains control is dangerous. They may still not listen."

"They won't if they assume Gettir is as greedy as they are." Before Finlay could protest Ogren added, "I am still willing to fight them."

"At least wait until after dinner. But if your plan works . . . ."

"A miracle," Ogren said, meaning it.

"In the meantime I'll prepare my spells in case we can catch Gettir's heart as securely as you say."

THE NOTHINGNESS BELOW THE CASTLE was still growing. Luckily for Ogren, though, so was his master's staircase.

"You have betrayed your oath," Gettir whispered, though his voice lacked anger as he gazed around at the heads of the great houses, then let his eyes fall limp on his bodyguard. For the first time, Ogren realized what people meant when they said they would have rather someone they cared about screamed at them than gone silent.

"Impossible, sire," Ogren said. "I brought the wizards with me to testify to the truth of our plan. If you are willing. If not, they will leave."

"And then attack my castle," Gettir said.

"But," Finlay replied, "we *will* leave first. Will you hear us out, master?"

The Sire Wizard smiled thinly. "You always did ask politely, Finlay."

In the end, Gettir did agree, on the condition that Ogren be allowed to stay — which had been one of Ogren's conditions, if not an outright necessity, anyway.

And so it went with the six wizards surrounding Gettir's bed: Not the *Lacere* but something altogether different, wholly new, untried and untested, as graceful as a hurricane, as colorful as a volcano, as quiet as a lion. Ogren felt the power like ice pellets against his face until his cheeks were hard and numb and his eyes clouded. And Finlay had warned him each second was only a drop to Gettir's ocean.

Finlay was the closest to Gettir and charged with the gravest task of all despite his youth: Instead of dispersing the magic as a normal *Lacere* would, he channeled it by use of his story-spells: weaving tales that wove castings which he then gave to the wizards, who formed an oval human chain with each wizard accepting a particular task. Taillade the Elemental dispersed the great energy toward its dual destinations while the others prepared the way: They rebuilt Mount Zerubal first, its memory still so recent the air itself remembered how to piece it back together, along with the castle and the surrounding land that had fallen away into neverness. Then Sophia called the winds to clear away the layers of waste from Moravan and the tops of the dunes from Yakika, while the others . . . Ogren wasn't certain what all of the others were up to, and he had little inclination to ask.

And Ogren himself . . . standing by in case the magic erupted out of control. He would touch anyone at risk, thus making them immune. He already knew, he morbidly admitted to himself, that he would save Finlay first if more than two of the wizards were endangered at once.

At last, as suddenly as a storm transforming into a cloudless blue sky, it was done. "Quickly!" Finlay whispered to Ogren, who was already taking Finlay's bedside seat as the Wizard of Stories abandoned it. Gettir's eyes were smoky glass and Ogren felt as if he were watching Gettir's mind and soul departing like silent snowfall melting silently before touching the earth.

"It is all gone," Gettir muttered.

Ogren lifted the old wizard's head in his hands. "Sire, tell me about Yakika. Before it was a desert."

The white brow trembled. "Yakika . . . ?"

"When it was a fertile prairie. Tell me the oldest, farthest story you remember."

Ogren was vaguely aware of Panchere, the Star-Bearing Wizard, hovering over them — literally — but paid little mind to anything but Gettir's eyes, which now moistened with tears his body found an effort to produce. "I am no longer a wizard, Ogren," he said.

"But you are a storyteller, Gettir. With the longest memory in the world."

Ogren felt Panchere's magic lift and carry them away like riding a swing hanging from the Creation Tree at the center of the world. Sunlight beamed down on them and wind stirred the golden grasses engulfing them and the ruins of stone houses and shops uninhabited for centuries, sand-blasted by dunes that rolled for centuries until halted a few hours before. "Whose magic is this?" Gettir asked.

"Yours, sire," Taillade said.

"Sire," Finlay cut in, "that square building over there built of greenstone with the windows shaped like oak trees . . . Who crafted such a thing, I wonder?"

Gettir's eyes lit up. "Ah, that piece of work belonged to the Overmagistrate Arnham! He was quite a petty little man, really, but he had a delicious mind for architecture. In fact I was the one who suggested to him the shape of the windows, and I first laid eyes upon that house the day after the cornerstone was laid, which was the same afternoon the Lady Maggie True sang her first poem in this very town's Wildfire Inn . . . ."

As he spoke, Finlay cupped one hand toward the old man, gathering the story as he would grains of sand, then his other arm outstretched and the hand opened, sending those grains sailing into the wind.

While Ogren watched, the sandblasted stones of the ancient inn lost their wear and filled out to round fullness again; the roof reconstructed itself as Gettir remembered it; glass panes in the windows formed from the sand below the once-gaping holes; at last, a fire sprung up in the hearth and flowers blossomed along the front of the southern side of the structure. A memory turned story turned seed for the reblooming of a dead land, whose death would not be forgotten but soon, would no longer be visible.

"DECHIRER HIMSELF HAS BEEN ASKED to write the treaty," Finlay told Ogren the following evening. "Mediated by the heads of the wizarding houses. Within a few months both Yakika and Moravan will be fertile enough to settle and farm — with the treaty allowing citizens of any land to live in those places, our overcrowding should be a thing of the past. At least for another century or so, but I'll give the matter some thought. Will you and your men be staying with the Sire Wizard, Ogren?"

"Of course my men and I are staying on," Ogren snapped, feeling testy for a reason he couldn't quite pin down. "Our oath to Gettir remains, magic or no magic. An army of bards is hardly a rock-wall military force, even if they do surround him at all hours of the day."

"Your voice carries a tatter of jealousy, master warrior. Why is that?"

"Why should I be — " He was cut off by a warning bell clanging in the back of his mind that any denial would be a lie. "It seems — odd, Master Finlay, that the world has come to Gettir's doorstep again after so many years. That his stories . . . ."

"Are told to far more ears than yours alone? It's not as if he's abandoned you, Master Ogren. In fact I'll bet you'll still be closer to him than any of us for whatever time Gettir has left. Though you'll have to share him with me from time to time while I draw memories out of him — particularly as his mind fails more."

Ogren grunted, not quite capable of affirming or denying Finlay's guess. It went deeper than that, though. Ogren had not a single clue as to who his parents were or what sort of childhood he'd known. Gettir, with his stories and with his paternal eye over Ogren and the other Peleshtam, and his greater interest in Ogren for things beyond military skill, made the old ex-wizard the only father figure Ogren had ever known.

"You realize we're in your debt," Finlay eventually, gently interrupted Ogren's thoughts. "What payment would you ask of us? We have plenty of gold to go around."

"Not gold — at least not for me," the warrior told him. "I want you to draw memories out of *me*, Master Wizard. There are a great many pieces missing from my life, and I would have you fill them in for me."

"Tonight, then? After Gettir retires — "

"Not tonight. Perhaps not even this season. But you'll hear my call." *Before Gettir leaves us. For once, I would enjoy telling* him *a story*.

Having waited his whole life, Ogren thought it wouldn't hurt him to wait a little longer. But more than that, an innate voice within the shadows of his brain told him that great stories awaited unveiling. Ogren wanted to make perfectly certain he was ready when it came time to catch the wind.

Leah Bobet
Letters to Papa

for C.M. and J.T.

We post our letters on Sundays
at the box on the riverdock
photos and postcards and *wish you were here*
on the barge, 'cross the river, to Papa's place.
The shops sell candy and gold stamps, dockside:
crinkled, soft with foil, each heavy as a year
of news and tidings, of grief and joy,
another year of *wish you were here.*

We take home his bone-paper letters Sundays
with his photos bleached bare by the river wind
How are you? *The same.*
How's your back now? *The same.*
Tell your mother I love her;
our love is the same.
His handwriting loops like funeral flowers
beautiful, rare; red ink strong and clear.

She never writes 'cross the river, not far from our town,
where the carnival masks bob and leer through the streets.
She sits in the car until Sunday sundown
And we urge her to read as the stars all come out
as the sugar-joy fades and the darkness steals out.
No, she says tight, mouth pulled down, mourner's frown
Our love is not the same at all.

Lawrence Schimel
Winter Day

> " . . . a basket of wine and cake
> to take to her grandmother
> because she was ill.
> Wine and cake?
> Where's the aspirin? The penicillin?"
>> — Anne Sexton, "Little Red Riding Hood"

Looking for you among these rows of curtained beds
I feel lost as in a wood, not a hospital ward.
A nurse stops me, asks where I am going.
She directs me to this room, but this is not your face
I see on the pillow, so pale now, a fuzz of hair
all that's left after chemotherapy. Your eyes
look huge behind coke-bottle glasses. "Come closer,"
you whisper. "I've got CMV in that eye."
I've brought you a basket of your favorite foods.
I know your appetite is gone these days, but let me believe
it's only because of the hospital fare.
I need someone to blame for what's happened to you.
If I close my eyes, your lovers (at least, the ones I'd met)
parade before my eyes; which of them deserves reproach?
Which of them is still alive? Do you even know?
I start to ask you about Marvin, who shaved his legs
        and chest
and wore women's clothes I could only dream of ever
        fitting into.
You shiver beneath the thin hospital sheets and my
        condemnations
dissolve, unuttered. I look for blankets. I can't find any,

so I take off my coat and tuck it around you for warmth.
The red hood sits upon your belly as if you were pregnant,
and you laugh. "That's how it would have been," you say,
meaning, of course, if you and I had married like we
        always said we would,
back when we were best friends in college and I still
        sometimes thought
a girl like me stood a chance with a boy like you.
The nurse comes in to give you a shot and sends me out.
Downstairs, through a window, I see snow has begun
        to fall.
I've left my coat up in your room, but I don't go back for it.
You need it more than I. It seems the least I can do.

About the Authors

Danny Adams is the co-author, with Philip Jose Farmer, of the short novel *The City Beyond Play*, forthcoming from PS Publishing. His shorter work has appeared or is forthcoming in *Abyss & Apex*, *Ideomancer*, *Mythic Delirium*, *Not One Of Us*, *Paradox*, *Star*Line*, *Strange Horizons*, and *Weird Tales*. He lives in the Blue Ridge Mountains of Virginia.

Mike Allen's previous projects as an editor of fiction and /or poetry include *New Dominions: Fantasy Stories by Virginia Writers* ('95), the webzine *Event Horizon* ('96 to '98), and the poetry magazine *Mythic Delirium* ('98 to now). More recently, he co-edited *The Alchemy of Stars: Rhysling Award Winners Showcase*, which collects the Rhysling Award-winning poems from 1978 to 2004 in one volume. He lives in Roanoke, Va., with his wife Anita, two comical dogs and a demonic cat. His website is www.descentintolight.com.

Helena Bell is a graduate student at Southern Illinois University where she is pursuing an MFA in poetry. Her poems have appeared in *Strange Horizons*, *Ideomancer*, and *Jabberwocky II*.

Leah Bobet lives in Toronto, where she studies Linguistics and works in Canada's oldest science fiction bookstore. Her work has appeared in *Science Fiction: The Best of the Year 2006*, *Strange Horizons* and *Realms of Fantasy*.

Deborah P Kolodji works in information technology to fund her poetry obsessions. The author of four chapbooks, her work has appeared in *Modern Haiku*, *Strange Horizons*, *Mythic Delirium*, *Scifaikuest*, *Frogpond*, *bottle rockets*, *Star*Line*, *Dreams and Nightmares*, *Abyss &Apex* and *The Magazine of Speculative Poetry*.

Richard Parks lives in Mississippi with his wife and three cats. PS Publishing will bring out his novella, *Hereafter and*

After, as a signed limited edition in late 2006. His second story collection, *Worshiping Small Gods* (Prime Books), is set to launch at the World Fantasy Convention in Austin. Richard claims that "A Pinch of Salt" was inspired by Neil Gaiman, but it would take too long to explain why.

Cherie Priest is the author of *Four and Twenty Blackbirds*, a southern gothic novel with two sequels in the works from Tor Books. She's also working on a mosaic novel called *Dreadful Skin* — which will be available early next year through Subterranean Press.

Charles Saplak has published fiction and poetry in numerous magazines and anthologies. When not writing he likes gardening and woodworking. He can be reached at saplak@verizon.net. This is the first U.S. publication of "Visanna."

Lawrence Schimel is a full-time author, anthologist, and translator who has published over 80 books, including *The Drag Queen of Elfland*, *His Tongue*, *Two Boys in Love*, *Things Invisible to See: Lesbian and Gay Tales of Magic Realism*, *The Future is Queer*, and others. His poem "How to Make a Human" won a Rhysling Award and his anthology *PoMoSexuals* won a Lambda Literary Award. He lives in Madrid.

Ekaterina Sedia lives in Southern New Jersey with the best spouse in the world, two needy cats, and many other life forms. Her short stories sold to *Analog*, *Dark Wisdom*, *Surreal*, *Fantasy Magazine*, and *Spicy Slipstream Stories*. Her novel, *According to Crow* (Thomson/Gale), was published in May 2005. Visit her website at www.ekaterinasedia.com

Sonya Taaffe has a confirmed addiction to myth, folklore, and dead languages. Her poem "Matlacihuatl's Gift" shared first place for the 2003 Rhysling Award, and a respectable amount of her short fiction and poetry was recently collected in *Postcards from the Province of Hyphens* and

Singing Innocence and Experience (Prime Books). She is currently pursuing a Ph.D. in Classics at Yale University. She says the source material for "The Marriage of Iphis and Ianthe" can be found in Ovid's Metamorphoses 9.666—797 and "Homecoming" in the Odyssey.

Steve Rasnic Tem has collected a small portion of his over 250 published short stories in the collections *City Fishing* (Silver Salamander) and *The Far Side of the Lake* (Ash-Tree Press). He is a past winner of the World Fantasy, British Fantasy, Bram Stoker, and International Horror Guild awards. A volume of his selected poetry, *The Hydrocephalic Ward*, has been published by Dark Regions Press.

Sheree Renée Thomas is a Memphian in New York. Her short stories and poetry appear in *Southern Revival, Strange Horizons, ESSENCE, storySouth, Mojo: Conjure Stories*, and *So Long Been Dreaming: Postcolonial Science Fiction & Fantasy*. Look for new work in *Mythic Delirium, Hurricane Blues, Bronx Biannual, The Ringing Ear*, and *Callaloo*.

Catherynne M. Valente writes novels and poetry and occasionally deconstructs Greek plays for fun and profit. Her novels include *The Labyrinth, Yume no Hon: The Book of Dreams, The Grass-Cutting Sword* (all from Prime Books) and, forthcoming from Bantam/Dell in November, *The Orphan's Tales*. Her poetry books include *Apocrypha* and *Oracles*. Her website is http://www.catherynnemvalente.com/

JoSelle Vanderhooft is a Utah-based poet, novelist and freelance writer. Her books include *10,000 Several Doors, The Tale of the Miller's Daughter* and *Desert Songs* among others. Her poetry and short stories have appeared or will appear online and in print in *Star*Line, Cabinet des Fées, Sybil's Garage, Mythic Delirium, The Seventh Quarry* and others. She'll see a chapbook from Cross Cultural Communications published in the fall, and her novel *Owl Skin* is due out in December.

Jo Walton's latest novel is *Farthing*, an alternate history mystery. She has won the World Fantasy Award (for *Tooth and Claw*) and the John W. Campbell Award. She comes from Wales but lives in Montreal where the food and books are more varied. She writes that her poem was inspired by Elise Matthesen in online conversation.

Erzebet YellowBoy's short stories have appeared in *Fantasy Magazine*, *Jabberwocky 2* and *MYTHIC* and her poetry is forthcoming in *Mythic Delirium*. Her first novel, *Sleeping Helena*, will be released by Prime Books in Spring, 2007. She is the founder of Papaveria Press and co-editor of *Cabinet des Fées*, a journal of fairy tale fiction and in her spare time, she plays with bones. Her website is http://www.erzebet.com